# Spotless

# HOME

# BAILEY BRADFORD

Home
ISBN # 978-1-78430-271-9
©Copyright Bailey Bradford 2014
Cover Art by Posh Gosh ©Copyright October 2014
Interior text design by Claire Siemaszkiewicz
Totally Bound Publishing

Published in 2014 by Totally Bound Publishing, Newland House, The Point, Weaver Road, Lincoln, LN6 3QN, United Kingdom.

Totally Bound Publishing is an imprint of Total-E-Ntwined Limited.

*Totally Bound Publishing books by Bailey Bradford:*

Breaking the Devil
Dark Nights and Headlights
Texas and Tarantulas

## Southwestern Shifters
Rescued
Relentless
Reckless
Rendered
Resilience
Reverence
Revolution
Revenge

## Southern Spirits
A Subtle Breeze
When the Dead Speak
All of the Voices
Wait Until Dawn
Aftermath
What Remains
Ascension
Whirlwind
Reluctance

## Love in Xxchange
Rory's Last Chance
Miles to Go
Bend
What Matters Most
Ex's and O's
A Bit of Me
A Bit of You
In My Arms Tonight
Where There's A Will

## Leopard's Spots
Levi
Oscar
Timothy

Isaiah
Gilbert
Esau
Sullivan
Wesley
Nischal
Justice
Sabin
Cliff

## Mossy Glenn Ranch
Chaps and Hope
Ropes and Dreams
Saddles and Memories
Fences and Freedom
Riding and Regrets
Broncs and Bullies

## Yes, Forever
Yes, Forever: Part One
Yes, Forever: Part Two
Yes, Forever: Part Three
Yes, Forever: Part Four
Yes, Forever: Part Five

## Spotless
Hide
Hunt
Home

## What's his Passion?
Unexpected Places

# HOME

# Dedication

To great friends, to family. I love you all.

# Prologue

*Five years earlier*

Solomon was in shock, though he did his best to hide it. He'd never expected to be rescued, had never thought anyone would free him and his siblings from their evil, sadistic father. Now they were not only freed, but their father, Bashuan, was dead, and the lepe or clan of snow leopard shifters he'd led were on their own. No one wanted to rule them.

Solomon wanted to forget they existed. Not one of them had put a stop to the beatings and torture he, his brothers and sisters had suffered. No one had wanted to help the half-breeds and risk Bashuan's wrath.

The sudden pressure of a hand on his shoulder startled him. Solomon couldn't quite control his reaction, flinching and pulling away.

"Sorry."

He glanced over to see who was speaking, and found that his newly discovered brother, Steven, was standing beside him.

Solomon wanted to look away. There was something about Steven that unnerved him. It could have simply been that Steven was a stranger even if, as it turned out, he was another one of Solomon's half-siblings. Or it could have been that the hard look in Steven's eyes reminded him entirely too much of Bashuan.

Except Steven didn't, not when Solomon finally settled his gaze on Steven's. There was warmth in his entire expression, and also what might have been nervousness.

How could a big, strong man like Steven suffer from a case of nerves?

That too was hard for Solomon to see. He averted his gaze, searching out Erdwin and Rhea as they approached.

"They seem close," Steven murmured.

Solomon swallowed, trying to work up the courage to speak. His entire world had just been altered, and processing it all was proving to be impossible just then.

"Solomon, where are we going now?" Rhea asked, running the last few yards.

Solomon opened up his arms. Rhea was sweet and mostly unharmed by Bashuan. She cuddled right into his body. "We're going somewhere safe," he promised her.

Erdwin, who was so thin and small he looked younger than his thirteen years, beamed at him. "Solomon never lies to us, so you know it's true."

"Solomon takes care of us," Rhea said. "Always."

The claim both bruised and soothed his heart. That childish innocence, the faith Rhea had in him, it made Solomon feel like he could take on the world—ah, but he knew better, didn't he? Bashuan had kept him and his siblings prisoners, after all.

But Solomon had vowed long ago to do whatever he had to in order to keep his family safe. Bashuan's death did not negate that vow in any way.

"Always have, always will," he assured Rhea and Erdwin and, perhaps at least a little, himself.

Solomon glanced over at Steven. "Always. I take care of them." It was a challenge, even though Solomon didn't realize it as such until the words were out. It was then that he knew he wasn't letting this stranger, no matter what Steven had done for them, come in and take control.

After studying Solomon for a long moment, Steven nodded.

Solomon did too. He hoped Steven got the message.

# Chapter One

*Present day*

"I don't want to help with the dishes," Rhea said, stomping her foot. With her bottom lip pushed out and those big blue eyes of hers, she got her way entirely too often.

If her current tendency to throw a hissy didn't get curbed quickly, then there'd be a world of trouble from her in another few years. Solomon pointed toward the kitchen. "I suggest you help with the dishes like you're supposed to if you ever want to see your Nintendo 3DS again."

Her pretty eyes rounded. "You wouldn't!"

Solomon arched one eyebrow at her. "Care to bet your 3DS on that?"

Rhea stomped her foot again. "You used to be nice!"

"So did you," Solomon told her, keeping his voice level. His intention wasn't to hurt Rhea, only to make her aware of how she was behaving, or misbehaving, as it were. Parenting was hard. Parenting sixteen siblings? Sometimes that was a nightmare—not that

Solomon would ever walk away from his responsibilities.

"I think she should have dish duty for the next month."

Solomon just barely kept from stomping his own foot at Steven's suggestion.

"I hate you!" Rhea yelled before pivoting and running into the kitchen.

"Not helping," Solomon snarled as he turned to Steven. "I had it under control."

Steven held both hands up. "Calm down. I was only trying to help. You're right. I shouldn't have butted in. It's just..." He sighed heavily and rubbed his brow. "She used to be so sweet, and now she's... That." Steven gestured in the direction of the kitchen. "I don't get it. It's like aliens took over one night while she was sleeping."

Solomon chuckled and felt his irritation drain away. "She's not the only one who's had fits about stuff, Steven." The younger kids had been more prone to such things than the older ones, like Erdwin and those around his age. "I think they've forgotten most of the bad that was done to them, and they're probably as close to normal as any kid can be. Hence, the fits. Most parents have to put up with them."

Cole and Shaun joined Steven and Solomon, with Cole shaking his head. "My dad could just look at you and make you behave."

"Your dad is the most powerful shaman in existence," Solomon pointed out. "And his mate is creepy."

Cole barked out a laugh.

Shaun giggled but bobbed his head.

Steven grunted and crossed his arms over his chest. "Cliff isn't such a badass."

Cole hissed and lightly thumped Steven on the back of his head. "Language."

"That means you get to do all the laundry tomorrow," Solomon gleefully pointed out. That was the rule—curse and you had laundry duty. With so many people living in one residence, laundry was a never-ending cycle of hell.

"If you cuss again, that's two days," Shaun warned. "And trust me. You don't want two days of laundry duty. It kills the soul."

Solomon was amused by Shaun's dramatics. "You should start up an acting troop. Think of it—you could put on shows when the pack gets together for ceremonies. Oh!" Solomon bounced on his toes. "You could re-enact Remus and Cliff's big fight with the evil shaman!"

Shaun slapped a hand over his own heart. "Oh, my dream come true! To be on the stage—" Then he ruined his performance by guffawing like a lunatic.

"Maybe we spoil them," Steven said, returning to the original issue.

Solomon wanted to argue that they didn't. Lying wasn't something he was good at, however. "I want them to have everything," he admitted. "Starting with better behavior for some of them, so I suppose we need a family meeting."

Steven slid an arm around Solomon's shoulders, speaking as he did so. "First, we strategize."

"Yes," Solomon agreed. They'd learned to make sure they presented a united front and all when it came to discipline and rules, although Steven did on occasion screw that whole thing up. It was his natural tendency to lead, to be the boss or alpha or whatever, Solomon knew that. He also knew it wasn't in his own nature to let someone else run the show, not when it came to family. "We should get Kylie, Erdwin, Vanessa and Jora, too," he added. Now that those four siblings were eighteen, he believed they should be involved in the parenting if they wanted to be.

Steven groaned.

Shaun patted his back. "Now who's trying out for drama king?"

Steven gave him the stink eye. "I'm not acting. That's heartfelt dread I'm showing there. And I still can't get over Erdwin being eighteen already. He looked so little when I first met him. Are you *sure* you had his age right?"

Solomon snorted at the familiar question. Steven claimed Erdwin had to have been ten at the oldest when they'd all been rescued, but the truth was, Erdwin had been malnourished and it'd stunted his growth. Fortunately, five years of good food and safety had fixed that. "You know he's eighteen now. Stop stalling. We're doing this family chat. Besides, it's not so bad, having more people weighing in on..." Solomon didn't finish. It *was* harder having more opinions bantered around. "They should get a say. That's what we agreed originally."

"We were idiots," Steven said bluntly. "Why did we think, oh hey, we're doing all right raising this herd of kids—let's make it more challenging by letting each one that turns eighteen have a say in raising the others? And why didn't anyone tell us how stupid an idea that was? Everyone argues!"

If they'd had proper parenting themselves, they might have done things differently. Solomon doubted it, though. After all, Cole had had a good upbringing with Remus as his father. Cole hadn't spoken out against their plan.

Cole shrugged as if he knew what Solomon was thinking about. "Seemed like a good idea at the time."

They split up to find the four so they could have their meeting. Cole asked Remus and Cliff to come watch the younger kids, much to the delight of the children and their babysitters.

Everyone knew Cliff was the biggest kid of the bunch.

"Ten bucks says we end up grounding him," Steven said when Cliff shouted and twirled Mett overhead.

Solomon watched the big, scary-at-times shaman spin Mett like he was a toy. "You go right ahead and tell him he's grounded. I'll be here laughing at you."

Steven nudged him on the arm. "You don't think I could take Cliff?"

Solomon didn't see any right way to answer that honestly.

"Let's get this parenting discussion over with, I want to make lemon bars," Kylie said. "You two quit picking at each other."

It figured they'd had four siblings turn eighteen in the past few months, Solomon mused. That was the thing about having a father who'd been intent on mating with as many female shifters of differing breeds as possible. Lately, some of Solomon's siblings had been talking about trying to find out who their mothers were.

A niggling of discomfort when the subject was brought up always began burbling in his belly. He refused to examine why.

This was his family. Solomon wouldn't lose any of them. He couldn't think about right and wrong, couldn't let himself imagine women mourning their children stripped away from them at birth or shortly thereafter.

Solomon locked those thoughts away. They were new to him, and troubling. He'd spent years trying to make sure his brothers and sisters were taken care of and now, suddenly it seemed he was having doubts that he'd done the right thing.

# Chapter Two

The matter of mothers didn't leave Solomon's mind. It bothered him for weeks and finally he decided he was going to have to do something about it. His own mother was dead. He knew that without a doubt. She'd been one of the few Bashuan had bred with multiple times before killing. Solomon had a few siblings some would consider his full brothers and sisters. To Solomon, every one of Bashuan's offspring was his 'full' sibling. There was no differentiating.

But Solomon didn't know if any of the other women Bashuan had bred with were alive, and once the thought had occurred to him, it wouldn't go away. There were nineteen offspring of Bashuan left. Steven and Adal's mother was dead. Taking into account Solomon's mother's death too, that left approximately fifteen women who might be searching for their children.

Then again, it could be fewer. Solomon didn't know who the mothers were. There could be more than one child per woman, and the chances of each mother having been killed were very high, too. Bashuan had killed often. Solomon had no doubt that had included Bashuan murdering his own offspring.

Solomon kept wavering between panic at losing any of his family members and guilt that he was possibly keeping some of the kids from mothers who might love and want them. Though with the way Bashuan had raped many females to force breed them, there was also the possibility the women would not want reminders of that violence and hatred that had been dealt to them by Bashuan.

It was too much to work out on his own but Solomon was terrified of bringing it up with anyone else. If he were told that the right thing to do was to let go of some of his siblings, he didn't think he could do it. That made him very aware that he was lacking in the areas of nobility and doing the right thing. How was he supposed to teach the younger ones right from wrong when he was such a hypocrite?

All he'd lived for, always, was to take care of his younger family members.

He couldn't worry all the time. If he did, he'd break into a million tiny pieces. He'd feel lost and… He had to be strong. Solomon worked out when he was able to. He spent time playing and talking with his family. He kept busy, going to bed exhausted each night.

He didn't neglect his own needs fully, either. Level-headed as he was, Solomon knew he had to take care of certain things. So he forced his mind onto another subject, seeking out relief from his worries. He was young, healthy, and his thoughts went right to sex as he stood in the shower, soaping his skin.

Solomon leaned out of the shower, pushing the curtain aside. He stretched and grabbed the lotion he kept close at hand, by the sink. He took the container and opened it, then poured a good amount into his palm.

He set the bottle down and recapped it as best as he could with one hand. With his other hand, he fisted his cock and quickly spread the lotion over his length. Solomon liked the way the white lotion looked on his dusky purple shaft.

He gave himself a couple of good strokes then, without further dawdling, began jacking himself faster. He let his mind wander but settled on no particular fantasy. Just the idea of a mouth or hand or hole, that was all he needed. Since he'd not experienced the touch of another, not in a sexual way, Solomon's imagination was limited—not that it would slow down his already building release.

Solomon moaned as desire pulsed along with his cock and balls. He'd arched against the shower wall and mewled. What would it be like to have someone licking him, touching him?

*It'd feel so good, to have that for myself. To have someone to turn to—* Solomon pumped his cock even faster, thrusting his hips into his grip, too needy to take it slow and let the tension build. He wanted, gods, he ached to feel another person's skin against his, to hear moans and…to even be kissed.

Solomon jerked his cock with harsh, quick strokes, trying to recapture that feel of earth beneath him. He needed more, so much more than he could give himself. He wanted someone to want *him*. That was as enticing as any sexual fantasy he could imagine. Just thinking about another person desiring him was incredibly hot. *To have someone to turn to.* The thought kept bouncing around his head as pleasurable sensations spread up from his groin.

Solomon plucked at one nipple. He pinched it harder. "Oh gods," he rasped, thumping his head against the wall. "Gods. Just—" Another twist to his nipple, and Solomon's balls throbbed. He reached down and cupped them, touched the soft skin behind them.

"Ungh!" He shuddered from head to heels, rising up on his toes as spunk shot into the shower spray. Solomon kept working his cock until it was too sensitive for more, then he curled over and panted until his head stopped spinning. The orgasm gave him temporary relief, but it wouldn't be long until his worries came back.

* * * *

By the time night fell, Solomon was entirely too cross. No one needed to be around him when he was a surly mess. If he didn't get a handle on himself by morning, he'd have the older kids watch the younger ones, and take a few hours for himself.

Morning came and he knew, when he opened his eyes after a restless night, that he was going to be a grouchy man even with the help of a pot of coffee.

Unable to find any peace within himself, Solomon decided to exhaust his body with more hard work. "I'll be working on the garden-to-be," he told Erdwin and Kylie, who were going to watch the kids so Solomon could get outside and concentrate on the task he'd set for himself.

"You've been brooding," Erdwin said before Solomon left.

Solomon looked at his brother. Erdwin was soft-spoken, and as he'd gotten older, he'd also become more introverted. Solomon suspected that he knew why that was so, but wouldn't broach the subject with Erdwin unless it became a risk to Erdwin's well-being. Everyone needed time alone, and time to sort themselves out, that was what Solomon believed, and Erdwin wasn't unhappy or unstable.

Solomon didn't have all of himself sorted out yet, either, and he was twenty-two, or around that age.

"Solomon?" Erdwin asked quietly.

Solomon blinked and shook his head a little. "Sorry, too much going on in my head. I didn't mean to space out on you."

"Go on, maybe you need a break from all of us," Kylie urged. With her short black hair and freckles, she was as cute as could be. She was also more of a take-charge sort than not. "We can handle the herd. We've done it before, and you should really think of taking a weekend away for yourself sometime."

Just hearing her say that made Solomon almost dizzy with fear. "No, I can't do that." He turned and all but sprinted out of the door before she or Erdwin could nag or question him.

Outside, the sun was only a few hours in the sky and the morning was cool. The humidity was lower than usual, and with a steady, gentle breeze, the temperature was actually on the chilly side.

Solomon pushed back a chunk of his black and white hair when the wind sent it flapping into his eyes. He should have tied it back instead of leaving the shoulder-length strands loose.

His pale eyes tended to unsettle some people even though he'd been a part of Bobby's wolf pack for years now. With his black and white hair, and gray-ringed white irises, he was very different from the other shifters. Some of his siblings had similar traits, but not the combination Solomon had. He stood out and always would.

It wasn't unusual to be ignored by most of the other shifters in the pack. Solomon didn't complain. It was enough that the wolves had taken in him and his feline siblings, given them a safe place to live. No one was outright rude to him, but he thought he made them uncomfortable for the most part.

But as in anything, there were exceptions, and it wasn't long into his walk before he saw Vanda approaching. Solomon groaned internally. He longed to be alone for a while, not accompanied by someone who wanted to get into his pants.

"Hey, Solomon," Vanda said, waving with two fingers at him. The way her eyes lit up when she looked at him, and the scent of her arousal was always on her when she was near him—both made it obvious that Vanda wanted more than he did form their encounters. It unsettled Solomon, and today he was in no mood for it. "Vanda, I need some time alone."

Vanda stopped short, a few feet from him. She scowled. "I wasn't going to throw myself at you again, Solomon. You've made it clear you don't want to fuck, but I'd hoped we could be friends."

He felt like a complete ass. Still, there was her scent. "But you—" He flapped a hand at her, uncertain how to phrase what he wanted to say. "I can smell—"

Vanda rolled her eyes. "Bet you can't smell it now. You didn't have to be a jerk about it, either. And just because I think you're fuckable, that doesn't mean I'd push myself on you once you've told me no. There's this thing I have, it's called pride, and it keeps me from making a total idiot of myself. You should try it sometime."

Solomon recoiled from her angry diatribe, protesting, "I wasn't that rude!"

Vanda pointed at him. "Yes. You. Were. Last time I tried to talk to you, you wouldn't even look at me. I didn't say anything inappropriate either. I haven't since I asked you if you wanted to fuck and you turned me down. I get that. I'm not everyone's idea of attractive, but some guys like a girl with a shape. Some like a bone of their own. Whatever, I can handle it either way. What I can't deal with is someone being a douche because they figure they're so hot I can't control myself. My body might still get horny because of the way you *look*, but trust me when I tell you my brain and heart know better." She aimed her chin up then turned and stalked off.

Solomon watched the way the dust shot up from around her heels every time they struck the ground. Had he been an egotistical jerk? *Probably.* He'd been weirded out by Vanda asking him if he wanted to fuck a week or so ago. No one had ever come on to him, and she'd just…just tossed that offer right out there.

And Solomon, in his virginal primness, had overreacted.

He groaned and rubbed his hands over his face. He was such a tool. Vanda deserved an apology. Solomon peeked out from between his fingers. She wasn't that far away yet. "Vanda, wait."

Vanda huffed loudly but stopped, her back to him.

Obviously, she wasn't going to make it easy on him.

Solomon would do the right thing no matter how uncomfortable it was for him. He approached her with a confidence he wasn't truly feeling. "Look, I'm sorry. I was a jerk. I—" His cheeks burned hot with embarrassment but he forced himself to continue.

"I've never had anyone even flirt with me before you said—"

Vanda spun around, her eyes wide. "No one? Ever? Like not even a little?"

Solomon wished he could just combust and let the wind carry him off. "No. In case you haven't noticed, the rest of the pack doesn't have much to do with me and mine."

"You and yours?" Vanda scowled at him. "That's the attitude that causes the space between you and the pack, in case you haven't figured it out yet."

Combined with his current internal crisis regarding the mothers of some of his siblings, Vanda's information almost caused Solomon to melt down and curse, something he hadn't done, ever. He had to set an example, after all.

"Look," Vanda said in a gentler tone. She took a step closer and touched his forearm. "I'm not trying to be ugly about this. I understand now. You're a virgin—and I will pass on that, thank you. I like my lovers already broken in—and I freaked you out. Obviously you don't understand sex and sexuality or you'd know when I was and wasn't trying to boff you. Let me clarify it for you—I have no interest in sex with you now, even if you are a fine-looking man. Hopefully that eases your mind some. As for the pack, just think about it. You have kept your family isolated for the most part, except when there are ceremonies and stuff like that. Are you doing all those kids any favors by keeping them apart from the rest of us?"

When Vanda walked away, Solomon didn't stop her the second time. He was too stunned by her revelations in regards to his lack of parenting skills. That he could have done his family wrong hurt him like nothing else could have.

Maybe he wasn't the best parent for the younger kids.

Maybe they needed someone with more sense and the ability to see and think better than he did. Someone not scarred by the past, someone who didn't want to cling so tightly to his family that he was possibly suffocating them.

Holy gods and Hades, what if he'd done it all wrong, all along?

Solomon's guts cramped and he started to fold over. What stopped him was the fear that someone else would see him and think him weak.

Or weird, weirder than he already was. Had he isolated his family? Yes, he couldn't deny it. He'd trusted only blood to keep them safe.

But it'd been blood that had harmed them all, in the form of their father.

*Dang it all, could I be any dumber?*

Castigating himself the rest of the way to the small plot of land, Solomon was bombarded with self-criticism and doubts.

Two hours of hoeing out a garden space didn't do enough to alleviate either of those things. Solomon's hands ached and blisters had formed on his palms. They'd be gone before sunset. Like any other shifter, he healed rapidly. Maybe faster than the pure-breeds, not that it truly mattered.

Being half snow leopard and half jaguar, he felt like an oddity. Except among his family, who were all half-breeds as well. All half snow leopard and something else.

Solomon stretched his arms over his head, working some of the kinks out of his back. He looked over the twenty-by-twenty foot space he'd been allotted by Bobby. Everything he needed was set out, from the chicken wire and posts for fencing to stakes to mark off rows of vegetables. Other shifters had gardens in their yards, but there was no room where Solomon lived. With so many kids, there were swing sets and toys all over the yard, wooden forts and even two large above-ground swimming pools.

And trampolines. Solomon really hated those things. It was a good thing he and his sibs healed so quickly, considering the numerous broken arms and legs, fingers and toes they'd gotten from those trampolines. Even with the netting around them, kids found ways to get hurt.

Solomon wiped the sweat from his brow with the hem of his shirt. Then he pulled his shirt off completely. Shifters as a whole weren't body-shy — usually. Solomon was. He had so many scars on his body, he hated for anyone outside the family to see him shirtless, or even wearing short sleeves. The same went for shorts. Solomon tended to keep himself covered up completely except for his hands, neck and face.

But he was hot, and no one was around. Solomon glanced down at his torso. There were two long scars that ran almost up the center from his belly button to his collarbones. He healed fast, sure enough, but not faster than Bashuan had been able to hurt him.

There were claw marks on his sides, then the rest of the places were smaller, albeit just as deep, and they'd all hurt horribly when they'd been inflicted on him.

It did no good to think on them now. He hated that his flesh was littered with his past. Solomon wanted to forget it all, but every time he showered, every time he saw himself undressing or nude, he was reminded.

And every time he woke up at night, a scream trapped in his throat, terror clogging his veins, his heart slamming against his ribs, he knew he would never be free. What had been done to him held Solomon in an iron grip, digging at him with sharp nails, reminding him how much he'd been hated.

Solomon wiped his entire face with his shirt then tucked the shirt into the back of his waistband. He started in on digging holes for the slender posts.

The sun heated his skin. Solomon wasn't concerned with getting burned. He had a naturally golden hue that would only darken. As he worked, he tried to focus on one problem at a time. The immediate, and easiest one to tackle, was integrating his family in with the pack better. Not only would the kids benefit from the additional companionship, but also, well... Pack members were more likely to defend them if they knew the kids, if they cared for them.

That was Solomon's reasoning, anyway. He hoped he was right. As to the issue about the mothers, he had no answer for that. How he'd even begin to discover who the women were, where they were...

An odd, prickling sensation came over Solomon. He stopped digging and turned suddenly, trying to pinpoint the exact cause of his unease. The area about twenty yards away that he'd had his back to was dense with mesquites and oak trees.

To the left lay the housing area where most of the pack lived, and to the right was more wilderness, as much as any land in south Texas could be called such. Directly in front of him before he'd turned was, eventually, San Antonio, but it was several miles off.

The domain belonging to the pack in that direction had been cleared somewhat, but for the most part, the majority of the land had been left to grow wild, as befitted the habitat for shifters. Solomon only got out in the wilder areas when he ran with his sibs, and he'd never encountered a human on the property.

Or a shifter that didn't belong. He'd also never felt like he was being watched before. He searched the trees and brush but saw no one and nothing suspicious. Still, when he turned back around, it was like an itch between his shoulder blades, that feeling of someone or something spying on him. Solomon even went so far as to put his shirt back on, in case someone was out there.

Even though the day wasn't particularly hot, he was growing overheated, working as hard as he had been doing. Solomon hadn't thought to grab any water to drink before leaving the house. His thirst, combined with the increasing surety that someone was out there, watching him, had him putting away his gardening tools.

Solomon wished he could shift and run, but if there was a human around that could see him do so, he'd endanger everyone. That meant the only way he could proceed was in his current form.

He still felt like he wasn't alone after he'd put everything away. Solomon faced the direction he intended to head off in. Maybe it wasn't a wise thing to do. It certainly wasn't cautious. Usually, he was cautious about everything.

But there was a tug at his core, and his nerves were hopping. Under his skin, between the flesh and tissue, he would have sworn an electric current flowed. Solomon tucked his hair behind his ears and started forward. If someone was out there, they'd see him coming. He was either a target, or...or something he couldn't put a name to.

# Chapter Three

Azil Echo watched the cat shifter approach. So far, everything was going according to plan—to everyone else's knowledge. Azil, on the other hand, was about to jitter right out of his body. He'd just be a lump of boneless goo if he didn't calm himself.

"He's approaching. We should have him in another two minutes," Balani said.

Azil heard his commander but didn't bother responding. Neither did the other three guards. They all had a job to do, and that was bringing the shifter known as Solomon back to Mexico. Azil was lucky to be allowed to even be a guard considering his gender. Males were hardly allowed any positions of importance. Hence him being the only one on this trip.

Azil got his mind back on track as he studied Solomon. There'd been so many scars over that honey-colored skin, it'd made Azil want to comfort the man. Not that he could, and he certainly couldn't voice his doubts about what was being done, or what was in the plans.

The other three shifters would be brought at a later time, if necessary. Azil didn't know all the details—he wasn't the trusted leader of the guards, but merely a foot soldier who had to follow orders.

Which was going to really fuck with what was happening inside him.

Azil had never looked at a man and wanted him. He'd seen such attractions between animals before, though no one spoke of such things. Even if he'd ever been interested in someone of the same gender, there never would have been an opportunity. There weren't any available males. All were owned as soon as they came of age. Only the fact that Azil was undesirable kept him from that same fate.

He *was* undesirable, though, with his fair coloring and orange hair. The freckles didn't help, either. Add in his height and bulk, and no female wanted to fuck him.

At least he wasn't an Outcast.

Azil's heartbeat accelerated with each step Solomon took toward him. They were upwind of the man, with Azil behind the female guards, so he scented them and, eventually, Solomon. No one could catch a whiff of Azil, which was good since he was, strangely enough, becoming aroused.

The female guards did nothing for him. Indeed, he was scared of them. In his society, women held all the power.

And now he was massively confused, because his dick was growing hard and he could smell that he was turned on. If he could, then so would the female guards as soon as they caught a whiff of him.

Panic made Azil's heart beat faster. He had a bad plan—bad because he was going to have to roll in something nasty to cover the odor of his pre-cum leaking from his slit. If Balani, Kacha, Oediata and Leeloo thought he was aroused because of them, they could gut him for it. Men had no control over their behavior — they were violent and dangerous if left to their own wiles, which was why women ruled in his clan.

He refused to think about the violence he'd seen the females unleash on others. He'd never give voice to the doubts, the ones that told him it wasn't a person's gender but their innate being that made them bad or good, violent or not.

Azil wasn't supposed to be an intellectual. He wasn't supposed to know how to read or write. He was just a slab of meat, a body to be ordered about. Had he not been ugly as sin, he'd be a body to fuck and be used.

He was definitely disposable, and so he must not let on that he was having a physical reaction to Solomon. It had to be Solomon, too, because not once on this assignment had Azil gotten an erection for his fellow guards.

That wasn't something he could wrap his mind around just yet. Besides, he couldn't take his eyes off Solomon. The man was taller than Azil's own five-ten. Surely Solomon was over six feet, and muscular, though not as bulky as Azil. Solomon's hair hit his shoulders, and was pitch black with streaks of white throughout it.

Azil wondered about that. Solomon was too young to have white hair. Perhaps he'd found a way to color it. To Azil's knowledge, such a thing wasn't possible. Then again, he lived deep in a rainforest, not in a big, modern country like the United States.

"You, stay back so you don't scare him," Balani ordered, unbuttoning her shirt until most of her breasts were exposed. "Leave him to me."

Azil bit his lip as a surge of anger shot through him. He curled his fingers against his palms, digging his blunt nails into the flesh there. The urge to reach out and shake Balani was unacceptable, and it scared him. Maybe he was wrong in thinking that unnecessary violence wasn't only a female attribute. He'd never felt so compelled to strike out at someone.

Azil shrank back, disturbed by the dark thoughts he was having. *Let Balani and her boobs do their magic. I'm just angry because...because...* Azil couldn't even put a finger on it. He moved back farther, until he was completely hidden by one of the old, bent trees.

His life had been pretty simple up until now. He knew his place in society. Even taking this assignment to another country hadn't altered that.

Then again, they'd traveled in the wilderness almost exclusively. Azil hadn't been around many other people. Even so, he knew he shouldn't be affected by Solomon like he was. Something was very wrong.

Azil had a moment of hope where he wondered if he wasn't becoming aroused from another scent, like perhaps Solomon carried a female aroma on him somehow, in his clothes or... But no. Solomon had been working outside, sweating, for hours. Azil smelled sweaty man, and it was going right to his dick.

"Maybe he won't look at Balani," Oediata whispered. "I wouldn't mind a roll with him."

Kacha smirked, but Leeloo ignored the banter. Azil wasn't surprised. Leeloo was also a new guard, and she had kept to herself except when she'd been directly addressed or ordered around.

Azil went back to watching Solomon. The man had a long, sure stride, and held his shoulders back in a manner unfamiliar to Azil. It took him a moment to understand that it wasn't the posture itself but rather the attitude with which Solomon walked that made him appear to be different from any other male Azil had seen.

Solomon was perhaps a witch, too, because he was entrancing Azil, who could do nothing but stare and try to breathe.

When Solomon neared, he slowed down and growled. "Come out. I don't have time for stupid games."

Balani purred, stepping out into a small clearing between the trees. She stroked a hand down her torso, between her breasts. "I have been watching you."

Her English wasn't horrible—all of them spoke it as a second language—but Solomon frowned as if he didn't understand her.

Azil caught onto what was happening just as Solomon made his move.

Solomon snarled and shifted in a split second, quicker than anyone Azil had ever seen shift before. He turned into a beautiful beast, as unique in his feline appearance as he was in his human one. Unlike in his human form, Solomon's hair wasn't striped with white, nor did he have spots like leopards did. He wasn't completely black-coated, however. The tips of his ears and tail were vibrant white. So were his eyes, except for the oblong black pupils.

He looked eerie and powerful.

Balani didn't shift. "Now," she snapped.

Solomon yowled and leaped, but it was too late for him. The darts struck him in the shoulder and neck, a quick one-two thud of impact barely audible.

"Get him. Use the chains if you must," Balani instructed as Oediata, Kacha and Leeloo scrambled forward. "Azil, you will carry him. That's why we brought you, after all."

Right, because he was the muscle and nothing more. Azil's anger seemed to be increasing by the moment, and he couldn't comprehend why. There was no reason for him to suddenly, thoroughly, hate his clan, and yet he did. He wanted to strike out, to remove the guards permanently.

He wanted them to stop touching Solomon.

It couldn't mean what he feared it did. Azil pressed his hands to his head and squeezed until it hurt. Even so, the distraction failed. He hated seeing Solomon being stroked and chained. It was wrong for the guards to touch him, to titter and tsk and judge Solomon's body.

Azil had to turn away. If he didn't, he was going to lose it and attack the guards—a sure way to get himself killed. He could take out one of them first, two if he was lucky, but there was no possibility of him killing all four guards. They were all too highly skilled to die so easily.

*What am I thinking? What am I thinking!* Azil was close to panicking. He wasn't aroused anymore either, which was a side benefit of freaking out.

He did avert his gaze until he was called over to pick Solomon up. In feline form, Solomon was big, too.

Azil ignored the other guards' comments as he bent to lift the unconscious shifter onto his shoulders. No one bothered to help him except for Leeloo, who silently hefted part of Solomon's weight.

"Thank you," Azil managed to say.

Leeloo nodded, her lips thinned into a flat line.

Azil wondered if she was mad, and if so, why. He hoped she didn't feel the same pull toward Solomon that he did. That would be too awkward.

"Let's go before anyone comes looking for him," Balani ordered. "We'll take him back then see if Shiba wants the others."

There was no reason for Azil to speak, so he didn't. He kept a steady grip on Solomon. Solomon's fur was soft and warm beneath his hands and against Azil's nape.

Leeloo kept pace beside him, which was unusual. She had that pinched look the entire hike back to the panel van.

Azil was worn out by the time they reached it. He was in good shape, but Solomon wasn't little and the hike in the heat was intense. Even so, Azil should have been able to manage it all better, but he supposed the chaotic sensations pinging around inside him were throwing him off.

Leeloo opened the back doors of the van. She also opened the metal cage, her frown deepening.

Azil wanted to ask her what was wrong. He didn't. It wasn't his place to inquire, and even if that barrier hadn't existed, he simply didn't know how to open a conversation like that.

"Let me help you," Leeloo said in a rough voice. She'd hardly ever spoken on the trip.

Azil wondered if that was why her voice sounded like she'd spoken over shards of glass in her throat.

They got Solomon down and into the cage.

"There should at least have been a blanket on the bottom," Leeloo muttered.

Azil agreed, albeit silently. He started to lock the cage.

"I've got it," Leeloo assured him.

Azil stepped back. He wanted to ride beside Solomon and hoped he'd be allowed to. He'd sat in the very back of the van on the drive in, although that hadn't been long at all. They'd only gotten the vehicle a day earlier.

But Azil's desire to sit beside Solomon was circumvented when Leeloo hopped into the back and took his spot. She arched an eyebrow at him, and for a moment, Azil thought there was some kind of amusement and maybe even hope in her eyes. She blinked, and it was gone, so he put it down to his own imagination.

Azil shut the van doors then went around to the side to get in.

"Leeloo, why are you back there?" Kacha asked. "There is a seat available."

"Maybe she's hoping to catch the half-breed's attention," Oediata said snarkily, glaring Leeloo's way. "There's not a chance of it happening, newbie. He is the property of our queen, and you know it."

Leeloo didn't even acknowledge the accusation. She merely leaned back and propped one booted foot on top of the cage.

"We'll give him another shot in an hour. I don't want him waking up and making a bunch of noise." Kacha took her seat. She pointed toward the back. "You, Azil. Get that way. If Leeloo doesn't want to sit up here with us, she'll just have to share the space with you."

Azil went around to the back doors again and opened them. He got in. Leeloo didn't help him shut the doors, but that was okay. She did scoot over a little for him.

He sat shoulder to shoulder with Leeloo but kept his legs bent, his knees almost pressed to his chest as the van bumped along the road. At some point, he noticed that the cage wasn't locked properly and he leaned forward to fix it.

It could have been a disaster had Solomon come to and that door not been locked. Azil didn't say anything. Leeloo was the one who'd been handling the cage, and he wasn't going to criticize her. Besides, she'd seen what he did. In retrospect, Azil wished he'd been more discreet about correcting her mistake.

Kacha came back and administered another shot to Solomon, then a third a few hours after that. They continued to keep Solomon unconscious for the twelve or thirteen hours it took them to get deep into Mexico.

Eventually, Balani parked the van in an isolated area and ordered them to drag the cage out.

Balani peered in the rearview mirror. "He'll need to go to the bathroom. He'll do it in the cage or not at all. We will wait here until he's awake then let him have some water. He won't be able to shift."

Azil didn't ask. He supposed it was something in the tranquilizers that kept one from being able to shift. Gods knew the clan's curandera was powerful enough to make something potent that could constrain a body to one form. *Permanently.*

Leeloo looked angry. She glanced at Azil.

He wished he could read her expression. She seemed to be waiting on him. "Do you—? I should lift the cage?" he dared to ask.

Leeloo rolled her eyes. She leaned very close, until her lips brushed over his ear as she spoke. "Do you like being a slave?"

The question stunned him.

"That's what you are. What all the males are. Do you think that's normal? Or right?" she continued. At the same time, she ran her hand down his chest, over his stomach, farther still, until she cupped his cock. "Does this make you property?" She squeezed.

Azil had no idea what was happening. "W-what—?" He gulped. Why was she still gripping him *there*?

Leeloo pulled her head back enough to stare him in the eyes. "Are you less than one of us, because of this?"

A second squeeze and Azil bit his tongue to keep from whimpering. Leeloo wasn't handling him gently. "Stop," he gasped when she added more pressure.

"Make me," she dared. "Fight for what you want. Don't just sit there and allow me to control you."

The doors were opened. Leeloo released him.

"Oh, looks like the new recruits are getting friendly," Kacha said. She hummed and looked him over. "Perhaps we should see what Azil is truly good for. So far all he's shown himself capable of doing is carrying things, and we could use a mule for that."

Cold dread settled in his stomach. He'd hoped to be left alone if he were allowed to be a guard.

"Isn't that why we have a male guard?" Oediata asked. "To carry and follow our orders? If we are on a long assignment and our needs must be met... That *is* why there are a few males allowed to serve the queen."

He darted an accusatory look at Leeloo. She'd done this, set the others to looking at him like he was a thing, instead of an— Well, not equal, never that, but something more than a body to be used.

"We haven't the time," Balani snapped. "Get the half-breed out and wake him. Leeloo, keep your hands off Azil until you're told differently. It's my understanding no one has had him yet and that means permission must be granted before any of us can fuck him. If you desire him, then request it first. While it's true males are sent out with us on occasion, it isn't always for sexual relief. Sometimes it is to do the grunt work. This would be one of those times, so I suggest the rest of you rein in your hormones."

"Are the other guards in place?" Kacha asked.

Azil was dizzy and nauseated from the pain Leeloo had inflicted on him, but he still startled at the question. He knew nothing more than the obvious about the assignment he was on.

"Of course." Balani tapped her foot on the ground. "Get. The. Cage. Out."

Azil realized she was talking to him. He banked his pain and ignored his queasy stomach. Leeloo got out and he followed, promptly grabbing the cage.

Solomon peered at him, those white eyes flashing in the moonlight.

Azil didn't even have time to process that before Solomon snarled and bit.

And all hell broke loose.

# Chapter Four

Whatever was going on, Solomon was putting a stop to it. He'd been feigning sleep more often than not. His captors had no clue as to his healing abilities. The scars might have made them believe he healed like they did. If they'd had any idea what Bashuan had done to him to inflict those scars, they'd have known the doped darts weren't going to cut it for long.

He didn't understand what they were saying. It sounded like they spoke some dialect of Spanish. In the end, it didn't matter what they were saying. He'd kill them all if he had to.

His senses were a bit skewed, his scent off and vision blurry, but he was awake when the male shifter grabbed the cage. The man wasn't bright, or he'd have been more careful. Sticking his fingers through the bars gave Solomon plenty of flesh to bite.

So he did—but the result wasn't what he'd expected. Righteous anger had been thrumming through him one second. Then he bit down, tasted blood and salty flesh—and his penis had twitched to full life, growing erect before the man's blood had even spread over Solomon's tongue.

His heart fluttered, his body went tight with need. Solomon growled, his cat brain and human brain struggling to accept what his senses were telling him.

*Mate. Mate!* He felt it all the way to his core, down to his essence, his DNA. Solomon was pissed off. His mate was this odd-looking man who'd helped kidnap him?

It had to be a mistake. The drugs were screwing with his head.

*His blood tastes so good. So good…*

The man didn't shout. He gawped at Solomon, full lips parted, eyes huge in his pale face.

"*Azil, o que você está fazendo? Pare de brincar!*"

Whatever the woman shouted, whichever woman shouted it, she sounded very angry.

Solomon sank his teeth in deeper. He saw the woman who'd sat by his cage reach for the lock on the door of it.

"*Deixá-lo fora. Parar morder,*" she snapped.

Solomon was fairly certain she was telling him not to kill or something like that. '*Morder*' might have had nothing at all to do with death, but her tone was laced with steel.

He growled at her.

She yanked the cage door open and thumped him on the nose.

Solomon sneezed.

The man jerked his hand back.

People started yelling—not the male—he remained quiet, stunned—but the four women were making enough noise to rouse all the spirits that might be sleeping.

The one who'd opened his cage door slit the throat of another woman.

Solomon knew then that everything was deadly serious.

And his cock was still hard, his body filled with a yearning he'd never experienced before. Someone ran at the man he'd bitten, waving a knife.

Solomon sprang into action instinctively, shooting out of the cage and tackling the guy before he could be stabbed. Assured that he hadn't killed him, Solomon bounded off after the knife-swinger. He hated death, hated fighting and fury, but not enough to lie down and die.

In seconds, there was only him, the woman who'd freed him, and the man he'd bitten left alive.

"Speak English," she rasped.

Solomon wasn't certain if she was asking him or telling him.

"Leeloo, what—?" The man snapped his mouth shut.

Leeloo wiped her bloody knife off on her pants. "What they are doing is wrong. All of the clan is wrong. They have taken my brother and—" She went silent quickly, too.

Solomon contemplated the duo. They didn't seem close. Both were still in human forms, though he could tell they were shifters. None of the people who'd taken him had bothered to morph into their feline forms to fight. It seemed odd to him, but what did he know?

"Azil," Leeloo finally said, pointing to the man Solomon had bitten. "He is Azil. I am Leeloo, of the Espirito clan, originally. Now I'm one of just two that's left of them, although I am supposed to claim only to be from the Vento clan."

Solomon cocked his head. There was much anger and bitterness in Leeloo's voice.

Azil—*what kind of name is that?*—was stocky and fair-skinned, with freckles all over as far as Solomon could tell. He had bright orange hair that went every which way, and eyes more of a mossy brown than green, though there was some of that color in them, too. He wasn't exactly attractive, with a nose too large for his face and thin lips, a jaw just a tad too sharp, and ears that would probably be standing out at ninety degree angles once all that hair was pulled back.

But he was attractive to Solomon. Azil didn't look like any male cover model Solomon had beat off over. He looked...unique and Solomon, who was unique himself, liked it.

Solomon didn't have a knife. He had claws and sharp teeth, weapons that Leeloo's knife wouldn't win against.

Yet he didn't attack her. She'd fought the other females, the ones who would have killed him. Or her. Honestly, Solomon wasn't sure why they'd fought at first. Eventually it had been a matter of survival.

Azil hadn't taken part in it.

Solomon looked him over. Azil seemed to be in shock. His eyes were wide and rather glazed. He cradled his wounded hand to his chest. Blood had soaked into his shirt. Solomon had bitten him deeply, had possibly even broken bones.

Leeloo held her knife up then tossed it blade first into the ground. "Shift. I am unarmed."

Solomon snorted at her. He still changed into his human form. "I'd hardly call a fellow cat-shifter unarmed."

"You are very fast. I can't change like that. None of us can. Is it because you are a half-breed?" Leeloo asked, raking her gaze over him. "Why is your penis erect? I am not letting you touch me."

Solomon's cheeks burned with a blush. "I don't want to touch you."

Leeloo arched an eyebrow and a smug grin pulled at one side of her mouth. "You are aroused by killing?"

Solomon grimaced. "Don't be disgusting. I'm aroused by him. Azil." He looked the man right in the eyes as he said it.

Azil gasped and scooted backwards like a rattlesnake was after him.

Solomon was only slightly offended. Mostly he was freaked out over that attraction, too.

Leeloo guffawed.

He looked at her. "What?"

"It isn't allowed in our culture," she explained. "Not the clan I am forced to be a part of. Was a part of." Leeloo glanced at the bodies behind her. "Now I will be hunted." She shrugged. "It doesn't matter. Wyanem, the queen of the Vento jaguar clan, killed my family, my clan, and stole my brother and me. We were to be the leaders, you see. Only my brother and I. The other children were slaughtered. She didn't want them. She thinks I don't know this, that I was too young to remember. I was only a year old, as was my twin brother. It matters not at all. We remember. I remember. She doesn't understand the power of a curandero's daughter. My father was very powerful, which is why he was killed through trickery. The queen, she is a fool. She doesn't see the death I will bring her for talking my brother and turning him into her sex toy."

Solomon didn't doubt Leeloo one bit. But, still— "What does any of that have to do with me?"

Leeloo huffed as if he had nagged for the answer. "She is your aunt. She is the one who sold your mother to Bashuan. Your mother, Irial, would have been the queen of the Vento clan had Wyanem not betrayed her. She has found out about you and your blood siblings. Nothing will stop her from owning you all. Killing you. Unless she can find a way to humiliate you and any other male offspring from Irial."

Solomon had believed his family to be safe, when really, they weren't. Had never been. "I have to get home." He pointed at Azil. "You'll come with me."

Azil flinched but bowed his head.

Solomon grimaced. "What's with that?"

Leeloo answered. "He is male. They have no freedom in the Vendo clan. They are raised to obey and serve, and taught they are of value only as breeders. Azil was allowed to join the queen's guards. He is stocky and can carry heavy weights, plus he would be used as a means of sexual release once the queen has the chance to take his virginity. She claims all the virgins," she added.

Azil hadn't spoken or looked up.

Solomon wanted to growl or curse, but he did neither. Instead he addressed Azil. "Please look at me, Azil."

It took a full minute, but Azil managed to look through his thick lashes at Solomon.

Like a punch to the gut, that look knocked the air right out of Solomon's lungs. "Gods. It's true," he murmured, amazement creeping in over the disbelief. "You're my mate."

Azil gasped. So did Leeloo.

Solomon slowly approached Azil, aware of how skittish the man was.

"My mate," Solomon affirmed. "I thought, when I bit you—but everything was happening, and I've never—" He was going to be tripping over his own tongue if he didn't get it together. The kind of lust he was experiencing was new to him. Solomon hardly had time to be horny, and masturbating in a house full of nosy siblings was tricky. To be flooded with such intense desire set his nerves on end and made him want to just fling himself at Azil.

Only the fact that Azil looked scared as all get out kept Solomon from pouncing.

"Mate?" he heard Leeloo ask.

Solomon got out an agreement, his gaze never leaving Azil's.

"We don't have mates anymore," she continued. "My true clan did, sometimes. Rarely. There are no mates in the Vento clan. Perhaps because they have bastardized the way relationships should be."

Solomon wasn't capable of engaging in a conversation with her about mates or clans. He wanted to touch Azil, and he needed to get home.

"Is there a cellphone to be had?" he thought to ask as he took another step closer to his mate. "I must get home."

"We don't use such things, and the van will not make it. We were almost out of gas, and Balani didn't fuel up since we were to abandon the vehicle here."

Solomon ran that over in his mind. He finally was close enough to touch Azil. The man was a good three inches shorter than him, and if possible, more innocent. It shouldn't have been possible—they should have been on even ground sexually, both of them virgins—but Solomon got the distinct impression that sex was something Azil had never thought much of, and man sex? Not something he'd heard of.

Solomon thought about sex quite often, and had been almost certain he would want a man for a sexual partner when he was able to engage in such things. He knew the basics of how to go about it all, too. Vanda hadn't turned him on in the least, but Azil— Solomon wanted to explore every centimeter of skin, wanted to learn to perform every lewd and every sweet sexual act he'd ever fantasized about.

But to start with, he slowly raised his right hand. "Can I touch you?" he asked.

Azil's eyes grew even wider. The man gulped, his prominent Adam's apple bobbing. Sweat trickled down the sides of Azil's face, beaded above his eyebrows, above his top lip.

Solomon could see the fast throb of Azil's pulse at the side of his neck, could smell the arousal wafting off him.

Azil held himself tense, like a touch might just break him.

"I'm sorry I hurt you," Solomon offered sincerely. "I wouldn't, had I known what we are to each other."

"We—" Azil swallowed again, then again. He licked his lips, leaving a glossy trail over them.

Solomon didn't mean to moan. The sound escaped from him as he stared at Azil's mouth.

A long moment of silence stretched out between them.

Solomon heard Leeloo off to his side, doing something. As long as she didn't interfere with him and Azil, he didn't care what Leeloo did.

"Can't you feel it?" Solomon asked after another minute. "The tug, right here." He pressed one hand to his torso, right below his heart. "It pulls me to you.

And this." Solomon ran a finger over the head of his dick. "I don't think it's ever been so hard. Are you hard?" He forced his gaze down and found a large bulge tenting Azil's pants.

"I'm sorry if I hurt you earlier," Leeloo called out. "I wanted you to fight what you've been told."

Solomon didn't like the sound of that. "What did she do to you?" he asked Azil.

Another loud gulp, then Azil bit his bottom lip before answering. "She... Sh-she grabbed me *there*, and squeezed. Hard."

Solomon risked looking away long enough to glare at Leeloo. "She touched you when you didn't want her to?"

Azil twitched one shoulder. "I didn't tell her no. I... I didn't... We don't say no."

"We?" Solomon's fury was building again, rising in him like a deadly weapon about to unleash itself on the enemy.

"Males," Azil offered. "We are property. She has the right—"

"Had," Solomon said firmly. "Even then, that is debatable. No one should be owned, therefore you shouldn't have been groped. Now, for certain, she has no right to touch you. No one else does, not even me, your mate, if you don't want me to. I will hurt anyone who violates you."

"Vio—" Azil's eyes actually bugged out at that. "I-it isn't— We aren't— I— She—"

"He knows no other way," Leeloo said. "And I will not touch him again. I thought the pain would jar him into independent thought. Instead I traumatized him, and I am sorry."

"You should be, and that isn't enough," Solomon informed her.

"Would me telling you that there are guards already waiting to snatch your full-blooded siblings help to make up for my mistake?" she asked. "There have even been murmurs of the clan curandera going along as much has been speculated about the shaman Remus."

Solomon sneered. "Let her approach him. Between Remus and his mate Cliff, who is also a shaman, there'll be nothing left of her."

Azil shrank back against a tree.

Solomon softened his tone. "She will be no match for my shaman. I don't think she could take on my brother Steven, or his mates Cole and Shaun, either. They are...powerful in a different way."

"Three are mates?" Azil squeaked out. He licked his lips again.

"That isn't possible," Leeloo added.

Solomon laughed. "It is too. Steven, Shaun and Cole, who is one of Remus' sons, by the way. They are all mates. We have many mated pairs and the one trio in the pack I belong to." And he really regretted not integrating his family into that pack better now. "Can I touch you?" he asked again.

"Yes," Azil said in a breathy way that scrambled Solomon's brain.

Solomon almost asked "Yes what?" until he remembered his question. He finally got the chance to stroke Azil's cheek, to feel the soft, warm skin. No stubble at all, and he wondered if Azil couldn't grow facial hair.

Azil's breath hitched.

Solomon froze, hand cupping Azil's face, desire coating him like a second skin, want flowing between them. He wasn't the least bit prepared for the sharp, startled cry Azil let loose with, or for the way the man lunged at him.

# Chapter Five

Azil didn't know what had come over him. It was all too much, everything. He couldn't think about it, was incapable of figuring out what was happening. He just...needed.

Solomon's hand on him, the scent and sound of him, the amazing white eyes, the intensity of Solomon's gaze—it all overpowered Azil's inhibitions, his fears. He surged forward, his own throbbing hand forgotten as need took over.

Solomon grunted and caught him up in an embrace that felt perfect. Strong, sure, Solomon pulled him closer.

Their chests bumped as Azil went up on his toes. He was very aware of his own erection, as well as the hot, hard length of Solomon's cock pressed alongside his.

Solomon was naked, gloriously nude, firm and sweaty in a way that wasn't gross.

Azil liked the smell of him, strong and tangy, musky. He clung as best he could with one hand injured.

Solomon wasted no time in slanting his mouth over Azil's.

At first Azil didn't know what to do. He pushed his mouth against Solomon's and fairly vibrated with need.

Then he felt it — the slick glide of Solomon's tongue. Azil moaned as he opened up, allowing Solomon to lick into him.

It was so good, being held. Azil couldn't remember anyone hugging him before. Solomon did it so well, and he caressed Azil's back and shoulders while sliding that agile tongue into his mouth, flicking it over Azil's.

Azil was so turned on he could hardly bear it. He dared to wrap one leg around Solomon's hip, and the pleasure that brought was incredible. Azil wasn't the only one who whimpered, either.

Solomon reached down and grabbed a handful of Azil's butt. He pulled on it.

Azil got the hint and thrust. He'd have sworn sparks shot out from his groin.

"Oh gods," he wailed, jerking his head aside. His lips ached, felt hot and swollen. His entire body was one live wire, ready to light up everything.

"Yes," Solomon hissed. He nipped at Azil's neck.

Azil couldn't help it. He came apart like a glass dropped on a concrete floor. One minute he was whole, the next he shattered. His body was taken over by a climax so powerful it blinded him as he came.

Solomon bit him harder. Azil felt teeth sink into his shoulder. The pain was fleeting, quickly changing to ecstasy that sent more cum spurting from his dick.

At the same time, Solomon ground against him, pulling Azil in even closer. It should have been uncomfortable, too much, but it wasn't.

Solomon stiffened, then cried out as he came. Azil whimpered as Solomon's spunk soaked through his pants.

"I suppose you are truly mates," Leeloo said. "That was interesting, and I don't care for males, so that's saying something."

Solomon pressed his head to Azil's neck. "I forgot she was even here."

Azil wasn't embarrassed, exactly. The women took the men in public, or anywhere they wanted to, in the clan. He had seen sex, many times. He'd just never been a part of it.

"I am glad to learn that mates truly do exist still," Leeloo was saying. "I had thought the world, our world, had become so warped, the gods and goddesses had taken that from us. Perhaps it is only the Vento clan that is incapable of having mates."

Solomon groaned. He pressed a soft kiss to the bite he'd made on Azil's shoulder. "Leeloo, please. If anyone is chatty after sex, it should be the people involved in the sex."

"I was involved. I watched." Leeloo chortled at that.

Solomon grumbled wordlessly then whispered in Azil's ear, "I'm sorry. I should have had more restraint so I could touch you in a private setting."

Azil shook his head. He didn't want to speak for fear of stuttering again. Sometimes that happened. It was part of why he preferred to remain quiet. "I didn't mind," he got out almost smoothly.

Solomon leaned back enough to give him a rather smug look. "You came harder than you ever have, I'd bet. You didn't mind, that's a bit of an understatement."

Azil surprised himself by smiling.

Solomon's amusement vanished as he stared at Azil's mouth. "That's a beautiful look on you, Azil. I hope you smile often."

Absurdly, Azil couldn't hold the smile in place then. He ducked his head and wished he wasn't such a mess.

"We need to move," Leeloo said. "We might be safe from the clan right now, but eventually, someone will wonder why we haven't returned. The way I figure, we have a week or so before anyone gets suspicious. If we had been traveling in shifted form, it would have taken a seven full days to reach the clan lands. It won't take as long to get back to Solomon's pack."

Solomon moved to stand with one arm around Azil. "And you are coming back with us?"

Leeloo cocked her head. "I am. I need the curandera dead before I take on the queen to free my brother. I also won't deny that I am hoping you will help me defeat Wyanem. I promise I will never lay a hand on your mate, on Azil, ever again. He is more entrenched in the way he was brought up than I'd realized."

Azil felt like an utter failure for that. "I can change," he murmured, not wanting Solomon to think him a loser.

Solomon touched Azil's cheek. "We're mates. Don't worry that I won't want you. Can't you feel what's already growing between us?"

Azil felt something, but he was afraid to trust it. "Everything seems too good to be true. To be free? I can't even figure out what that means to me. I don't know how to be free."

"None of the males from the clan do," Leeloo muttered. "You will learn."

"Who is your brother?" Azil asked.

Leeloo turned an angry look on him. "Can you not guess? He is Lotu, the queen's favorite."

Azil gasped, picturing the pretty man the queen frequently did things to—sexual things to—in front of any and all clan members. Lotu had the deadest eyes Azil had ever seen on a person. "Is it—?" He stopped himself before he could ask an improper question.

Leeloo studied him then shook her head. "I refuse to believe it's too late for him. If I can free him, and get him the help of a good curandero, or shaman—" She flicked a glance at Solomon.

Solomon nodded. "Remus is the best. One of his sons, Rolly, he is also an excellent shaman. Cliff is more of a, well, not a healer, exactly, but he is powerful, too. Then there is my brother, Steven, and his two mates. They are capable of things—Remus has said the Fates have a reason for bringing the three of them together. There is a purpose, a great purpose, for their triad."

Leeloo didn't answer. She went about gathering things into a backpack.

"Let me see your hand," Solomon said.

Azil had forgotten about it. He held it up and was surprised to see how quickly it was healing. "I usually don't heal nearly this fast."

Solomon smiled mysteriously then licked over the wounds. He proceeded to do the same to the bite mark on Azil's shoulder. "This, this makes you mine, Azil. Do you want to mark me in the same way? Do you want to...?" Solomon growled then nibbled a line up from Azil's shoulder to his ear. "Do you want to fuck me, sometime?"

Azil knew Solomon was embarrassed but pushing past it to ask him. Azil couldn't say how he knew that, but he did.

"It's the mate bond," Solomon whispered.

Only, Azil realized he hadn't actually heard the words spoken out loud. They had kind of just popped into his head.

*"You can feel what I feel, hear what I think when I want to share it with you, Azil. I can show you so much of my life."*

*"The scars,"* Azil thought before he could help himself.

Solomon wanted to shy away from that subject.

"It's okay," Azil said, feeling like a fool for having let himself pry.

*"I am ashamed of the scars. They're ugly, hideous reminders of a father who hated me and enjoyed hurting me. I wish they were gone, that I didn't see them and remember his hands on me, his knives, his claws, his teeth..."*

Azil hadn't known affection in his life, but he'd never known such cruelty, either. "I'm sorry," he said quietly. "I don't think they're ugly."

Solomon didn't argue, but Azil could feel his disbelief.

"Look at me," Azil urged. "I am unattractive. This isn't because of scars. I was born with this face, with this pale, freckled skin that burns. I am nothing like my parents, my siblings. It has saved me from being used yet by the females in the clan, but is that a thing to be proud of? I'm too ugly to fuck?"

Solomon growled loudly, an angry, fierce sound. "You are *not* ugly, Azil. You have beautiful fair skin, and I *like* freckles. Just because you don't look like everyone else in your clan doesn't make you unattractive, either."

"Your scars don't make you unattractive," Azil pointed out. He was about at the end of his comfort zone. While he meant what he had said, he had said more in the past hour than he usually spoke in a week.

"There are wipes in the van." Leeloo obviously wasn't interested in letting Azil and Solomon have a moment of privacy.

"We can shift and not worry about it." Solomon only waited a second then he let his jaguar take over.

Leeloo cursed. "How is it that you can shift? After all the drugs given to you, you shouldn't even be awake."

Azil looked at his hand. It was almost completely healed now. He touched his neck. That bite too was nearly closed.

He didn't usually heal fast like that. It wasn't in his nature. Azil thought of the scars he'd seen all over Solomon's torso. What kind of injuries could have left such marks?

Solomon was a glorious beast. Azil quit thinking and let his instincts take over. He shifted, a little faster than he usually was able to. That was cool and all, but what really struck him was how he felt his mind immediately mingle with Solomon's in this form.

What Solomon felt, Azil did as well.

Right then, Solomon was admiring Azil's thick, ginger coat. He truly liked it, thought the color was unique and warm.

Solomon purred and rubbed against him.

Azil whined, a meow-yowl that should have embarrassed him. Luckily, or perhaps not, Solomon stepped away. Azil could think a little clearer instead of just wanting to jump on Solomon and—

Solomon chuffed. *"If that's what you want, we can, when we stop to rest. In this form, or our human ones."*

And that was how Azil discovered what it felt like to have his penis hard in his feline form.

Solomon chuffed again, then trotted off after Leeloo.

# Chapter Six

"There were five of them," Bobby said, slapping his hand against a tree. Moonlight cast shadows all around them. "God damn it, how did this even happen? Where the hell did they take him?" he roared before anyone could even answer.

Steven seethed quietly. He was going to find whoever had taken Solomon, and tear them apart as slowly and painfully as he possibly could.

*"I'll help,"* Shaun thought.

*"Me too,"* Cole added. *"We'll get him back. He's going to be fine. Solomon is smart and he's a survivor."*

"The six of you, fan out and find a trail!" Bobby snapped, waving at some of his guards. "Move it!"

Sully murmured something to Bobby, but whatever it was, Bobby didn't agree, shaking his head violently. Sully frowned.

"Go get Remus and Cliff," Bobby directed.

Sully took off without arguing.

"Delio, go with him," Bobby instructed a guard. "No one is to go off alone."

Delio was fast, catching up to Sully in a matter of seconds.

Bobby turned to his guards and Steven, Cole and Shaun. "Whatever these shifters are, they used somethin' to fuck up their scents. I can tell they're shifters. Four females and a male. There was no blood spilled. What they wanted with Solomon, I can't figure. Steven, do you have any idea?"

Steven looked up at the sky. "It has to have something to do with Bashuan. What else could it be? Solomon was kept prisoner until we freed him. He can't have any enemies of his own."

"So someone lookin' to avenge a wrong Bashuan did them?" Bobby asked. "Or someone who just took the first of us they saw?"

"I'd go with the Bashuan theory," Cole said. "It feels right. I may not have all the power Dad and Rolly do, but I have some. This is linked to Bashuan somehow."

"Solomon has been worried a lot lately," Shaun added. "He's been off, I guess I'd say."

Steven looked at Shaun. "Yes. The possibility that there are mothers out there, looking for or wanting to know their children. He is afraid of losing any of his family. Solomon needs his security. We all know this. It is part of why the four kids that have turned eighteen aren't interested in leaving home. They worry it will hurt Solomon."

Bobby arched an eyebrow at him. "You know this for a fact?"

Steven gave him a cold glare. Alpha or not, no one questioned Steven's relationship with his brother. "I know Solomon."

"Cut the dickheadedness out," Bobby drawled. "I meant, did you know for a fact he was freakin' over the mama drama issue? Has he said why? Did someone try to contact him or what?"

One day, Steven might just have to invite Bobby to do a little scuffling. He wouldn't challenge Bobby for leadership of the pack—Steven sure as shit didn't want that job—but sometimes the alpha got on his last nerve.

Judging by the smirk Bobby wore, the asshole knew it, too.

"No one contacted him," Steven gritted out. "Solomon is just—"

"Intuitive," Cole murmured, tapping a finger against his chin. "He is. That makes me wonder if he's been picking up subconsciously on the subject. Like someone is seeking, trying to divine what has happened to a child or…" He shrugged. "It feels like there's a tinge of power in the air, too."

Steven sniffed, narrowing his eyes. He didn't feel it, but that didn't mean it wasn't there.

Bobby slowly pivoted around. "We need Remus and Cliff out here. Somethin' is wrong, and it's more than just Solomon bein' missin'."

Steven fisted his hands. He knew Solomon so well, saw so much of himself in the younger man. Steven had spent his life trying to protect his younger brother, Adal. Once Steven had killed Bashuan, he'd also discovered that he and Adal had several siblings.

And Solomon had been taking care of them all. Solomon had been horribly abused and more than half starved. He'd still been fierce and unrelenting in his position as guardian to all of the younger children.

For someone to have taken Solomon, that was a horrible blow to the family. Solomon had been their strength. Steven loved all the kids, but he wasn't as patient or as wise as Solomon.

"Call Adal and Dorso in to help. They can cut their visit to Colorado short for this."

Shaun was right.

Steven asked him and Cole to return to the house. "Not just to contact Adal but because we don't know what's happening. What if whoever took Solomon intends to take more of the kids?"

Cole paled. Then he turned and ran, with Shaun on his heels.

Steven hoped he was wrong, but the last words he'd spoken seemed to carry a heavy portent. Staying behind while his mates rushed back to the house was one of the most difficult things Steven had ever done.

"You think someone is coming after your family," Bobby asked bluntly.

Steven nodded.

Bobby started handing out more orders. "Jill! Take Gwen, Toby, Chris and Will back to the house. Guard it, and those kids. Call in the other half of the guards. We've got work to do, a pack to protect. I want that house secured, the people in it protected. Check the grounds, too, and I mean you look for anythin' even the slightest bit suspicious, you hear me?"

"Yes, Alpha," Jill said. "Move it," she told the others.

"We'll find him," Bobby promised, a fierce look in his eyes. "No one is hurting him. No one fucks with my pack. *No one.*"

For all that Bobby had just gotten on his nerves, Steven almost feared him then. It was easy to forget the power Bobby wielded, the strength he kept hidden beneath a layer of sarcasm and saucy grins. Bobby was deadly, and mean when he needed to be. He was a fair leader, gave out praise when it was deserved, and slapped down anyone who thought they were the gods' gift to the world.

"There's more to this than what we see," Bobby continued. "No signs of a scuffle, so I'd go with Solomon bein' drugged. Dart, most likely. Seems to be the method of choice for shifters to take each other out. Makes sense, I guess. So he was out here workin'. Got a lot done on the garden. Somethin' caught his attention, and he came this way."

"We found footprints!" one of the guards shouted. "Looks like the male shifter was carrying Solomon, judging by the way those prints are so much deeper in the ground."

Steven and Bobby ran to where the guard had indicated. They stopped at the first set of tracks.

"Someone tried clearing off the trail but they did a shitty job," the guard explained. "We're finding prints all over the place, leading west."

"Keep tracin' 'em," Bobby ordered. "I'm bettin' they used a vehicle, though. That's gonna make trackin' them harder."

"How much harder?" Steven asked.

Bobby didn't answer. He bent and sniffed at the impression left on the ground. "Jaguar. Isn't that what Solomon is, too?"

"Half, yeah," Steven agreed. He tried to catch the scent, but his senses, though acute, weren't on par with Bobby's.

"There are packs or clans to the south, and I mean Mexico and farther that way. There's one in Arizona, but I can assure you they don't have a hand in this. Someone is wantin' a goddamned war with us." Bobby stood straight and put his broad shoulders back. His smile made him look scary-mean. "They're gonna get a war. Won't be any of them left by the time I'm done with them."

* * * *

There was no peace to be had. Solomon was very worried about his family, and the pack as a whole. He also couldn't stop thinking about Azil. It was strange the way the Fates brought mates together. Strange, and wonderful, because Solomon, even while nearly drowning in his worries, was also content in that one area.

He had someone now, someone who would come to love him, who would support him and always be on his side. He wasn't alone, not like he had been. It was a wonderful realization and helped keep him from out and out panicking over the rest of the situation.

Solomon discovered that he wasn't in as good shape as he'd thought. After three solid hours of running, he was growing tired. It made him angry. He needed to get home, or at least somewhere he could get his hands on a phone so he could warn his family. No, he should call Bobby first. Bobby was his alpha. Then he could call Steven.

Another hour of running, then Leeloo slowed down. She led them to a cliff that overlooked a village of sorts. The ramshackle sheds were sparsely laid out. Solomon wasn't even sure anyone lived down there.

Leeloo shifted. It took her half a minute, and she panted for another thirty seconds when she was done. "I need to eat. We all do. I've burned up too much energy."

Solomon was confused by that. He shifted several times a day when he was playing with the younger siblings. So did everyone else he knew, and no one was exhausted by it. Then again, maybe Leeloo was referring to other things she'd done, before kidnapping him.

Solomon shifted, as did Azil. Solomon enjoyed watching his mate take his human form. Azil was barrel-chested but had no body hair except at his groin. Even his legs and armpits were bare. Solomon was kind of fascinated by that. He was on the fuzzy side in human form.

Leeloo began making her way down the cliff.

Solomon thought about telling her to shift again—surely it'd be easier in her feline form. But, she'd said she was tired, although not in those exact words. And she'd had to turn into her human form in order to communicate clearly with them.

The night was still dark, the moon having moved off behind clouds. Leeloo's darker skin helped her to blend in with the scenery. Azil, however, stood out with his pale coloring.

Solomon decided to shift anyway. He tried to shield Azil as much as he could as they made their way down the side of the cliff. Azil kept a hand buried in Solomon's fur for all of a minute, then Azil stopped and groaned as he worked himself back into his feline form.

Solomon really liked the way Azil looked as a cat. He was attractive in both of his shapes, though.

Azil chuffed and ducked his head.

Leeloo hissed at them both. "Hurry up."

The village was abandoned as far as Solomon could tell. The last human scents were very faint.

"Earthquake, two years ago," Leeloo said when she stopped in front of a pile of debris. "There weren't many people living here. Some of them were killed when their homes collapsed. The survivors took it as a sign from the gods to move, and so they did." She glanced at them. "I have learned a lot, traveling as a guard. Most people don't listen. They just do the job they're assigned and never think, never question. Never see."

Solomon was certain that last bit was directed at Azil.

Leeloo rubbed her eyes. "And I'm sorry to slow you down. I— The truth is, something is wrong with me. I tire easily. I ache inside. This shouldn't be happening, and I've hidden it for a long time, but it's growing worse. That's part of why I had to act now. I don't know..."

Solomon sniffed at her. She smelled like a woman. He couldn't detect any sickness, which meant nothing, really, since he wouldn't have known what every sickness in the world smelled like. Even so, shifters were hearty and generally, as far as he knew, disease-free.

Which made him wonder if it wasn't some sort of spiritual attack on Leeloo. He shifted, as did Azil.

"Has the curandera cursed you?" Solomon asked her.

Leeloo touched a spot on her side. "No. I have protection against that." She raised her arm and showed him the symbol carved into her flesh. "This. It keeps me safe from curses. Lotu doesn't have one. He was to receive his but we were attacked before it could be done."

"Do you believe he's under the curandera's influence?" Solomon asked.

Leeloo didn't answer for several minutes as they walked among the ruins. Finally, she stopped by a halfway-decent shack. "I think they may have killed his soul already. If so, all I can hope to do is free him."

It took a moment for her meaning to sink it. By the time it had, Leeloo was already lying down under the thatched roof, her eyelids closed.

Solomon hoped he was wrong about his interpretation. Surely Leeloo didn't mean that she would kill her own brother?

"Remus can help him," he found himself whispering.

Azil dipped his head down. "Sometimes there is no way to h-help."

Solomon took Azil by the hand and led him away from Leeloo. He looked for another place for them to rest. They'd need to hunt and find water, but first, a few hours' sleep was in order.

And Solomon's curiosity was piqued. "What do you mean by that comment?" He saw a place that might be stable enough for them to use as shelter. If not, they could always sleep out in the open, in either of their forms.

Azil sighed and followed him. "I've seen Lotu. The queen, she's done things to him—he has no life left in him. His eyes—" Azil shook his head. "I don't know that anyone can save him now. Leeloo may be right in that ending his suffering is the kindest thing to do. Or letting him end it himself."

Solomon didn't know why he felt so strongly about it, but he couldn't agree. "No. He needs to see Remus. We have to get Leeloo to promise to give Remus a shot at helping them before she does anything stupid. I thought she wanted to free him, anyway, not kill him."

"Perhaps they are the same thing to Lotu."

Solomon's mind reeled with that. "I was tortured for years, Azil. By my own father. I heal incredibly fast, which brought him much enjoyment, seeing how much he could hurt me. I've been—" He took a deep breath as memories flashed through his head, gruesome images he wished he could forget. "Chained

66

down while he took his time cutting me open. The agony is—it still haunts me. I can't even explain it, how much it hurt to have him slicing me, burning me inside just to watch what happened."

"Stop," Azil pleaded, grabbing his hands. "Please don't. If you have to tell it to...to heal some, then okay. But if you're just saying to—" Azil darted up and pressed his lips to Solomon's.

Kissing was certainly better than remembering. Solomon wound his arms around Azil and parted his lips. He canted his head for a better fit of their mouths, then sank his tongue in deep, tasting as much of Azil as he could.

Azil whimpered and wiggled, his hard cock already leaking pre-cum against Solomon's hip.

Solomon massaged his way down Azil's back to the taut, rounded globes of his ass. Those, he kneaded gently, pulling them apart, pushing them back together.

When Azil kissed him more ardently, Solomon shivered and squeezed Azil's butt cheeks. He needed to hold on tighter, what with the way his knees were feeling rather gelatinous.

Azil moaned and pushed his slick tongue over Solomon's lips. Solomon returned every thrust with one of his own. He was taller than Azil, but they worked together to make the most of their differences.

Solomon found himself nipping at Azil's lips and tongue, trying to imprint himself upon Azil. The feel of Azil's hard cock pressed against Solomon's body was addictive. Solomon wanted Azil to get off on him like that again, rutting and humping, spilling his seed onto Solomon's skin, and licking it all off—

"Yes," Azil murmured around a kiss. He canted his hips and jutted the wet-tipped length against Solomon. "Gods, yes."

But that prodding dick brought other ideas to Solomon's mind. And he suddenly had other plans for them. Other things he needed, ached for.

Azil began moving backwards under Solomon's direction.

"Down," Solomon stopped kissing long enough to say.

Azil gasped, no doubt picking up on Solomon's intention.

"Is it okay?" Solomon asked. "Is it what you want, too?" He knew just from what Leeloo said and from Azil's easy acquiescence that Azil could agree simply from his training. Solomon needed to be inside his mate, but he wouldn't do it unless it was something Azil craved as well. "What is it that *you* want?" He licked a stripe of salty skin beneath Azil's ear. "It's up to you. All of this, it's for you to decide."

Azil jerked his head back and gasped. His eyes went wide as he comprehended that he was the one leading their dance. Then he smiled, a sultry, sexy twist of lips that filled Solomon with so much desire, his blood warmed with it.

His own smile was likely more feral than not as he pushed Azil back.

Azil went down easily, kneeling first then lying on the red dirt. "I want you."

That Azil didn't stutter at all bespoke more of his need than the words themselves. Azil huffed out a sweet laugh that caused butterflies to flit about in Solomon's belly.

"I like that sound," he admitted as he knelt between Azil's spread legs. He'd waited his whole life for this moment, for merging with his mate and becoming one with him.

Maybe he hadn't thought a lot about it—gods knew he'd been busy raising kids—but that inner part of his soul had yearned. And now he needed, like he'd never have believed possible, and that chased away his nervousness at doing something he'd never done before.

"What sound?" Azil asked as he parted his thighs wider. "What did I do?"

Solomon looked into Azil's eyes. "Your laugh. I like that."

Azil's smile was every bit as good. He reached down and stroked his cock. "I didn't even realize." He rolled his lips in then blurted out, "Are you going to use me?"

Solomon's mouth went dry.

"No one else ever has," Azil continued. His nipples stood out on his chest as he inhaled. Solomon needed his mouth on those dark brown tips. "I am a virgin. I— I hated looking different, but I liked that it kept me from being...being used like...like... But you want me, don't you? I want you to want me."

"I need you," Solomon got out, eyes on that thick shaft again. "We can do whatever you want. You can be in me. We can touch each other instead. Could even taste each other."

Azil's breathing sped up. "Taste?"

The more Solomon thought of it, the better that idea seemed. Two virgins and no lube probably would not make for the best first time anal experience.

"Like this," he said before turning and placing a knee on either side of Azil's head. Without further talk, he reached for Azil's dick.

The fat crown was slick with clear fluid, and the skin was silky over the rigid hardness it covered.

Azil squeaked in surprise. Solomon lowered his head and lapped at the wide slit.

"Oh!" Azil kicked his heels against the ground. "Oh!" His hips jutted and he grabbed at Solomon's legs. "Oh my gods!"

Solomon grinned and sucked the broad tip in.

"Argh!" Azil yelped again and thrust up.

Solomon wasn't prepared for that, and gagged as the head hit his throat.

Azil tried to scramble away, but Solomon penned him in with his arms and knees. "Do you want to stop, or are you embarrassed?"

"I-I didn't mean—" Azil inhaled shakily. "It just felt so good."

"That's what I want to hear," Solomon assured him. "Now, back to this." He did use a forearm to pin Azil's hips down before suckling on the cockhead again.

Azil mewled then his breath gusted over Solomon's cock.

Solomon tensed all over, even clenching his ass at the sudden vision of Azil touching him there.

"You want that?" Azil asked timidly.

Solomon didn't answer out loud. Instead he sought out the mental link mates developed and let Azil see straight into his head, how turned on and needy Solomon was.

At the same time, Solomon palmed Azil's balls, giving them a roll as he sucked forcefully on Azil's crown.

Azil loosed a vowelless sound then he licked at Solomon's dick.

Solomon almost came on the spot.

Azil began lapping at him eagerly, then sucking.

Solomon had to really concentrate to remember to keep doing what he was doing. Azil had a beautiful cock, thick and long, veiny and delightful to discover. Solomon learned each ridge and bump, each spot that made Azil moan and try to push in deeper.

He kept after Azil's balls for a while before daring to move his fingers down to that tight little pucker.

Azil pulled off sucking him. "Please, please, please—"

Solomon would have answered, but Azil pushed a fingertip at Solomon's asshole just as suddenly.

Solomon wanted to thrust back and get that digit in him, dry or not. He felt empty and aching for it.

Azil moaned around the mouthful of Solomon's dick.

Solomon really loved the vibrations that caused around his cock, so he tried it as well, moaning loud and long when he had Azil's shaft halfway in his mouth.

Azil pulled off sucking him and keened.

Solomon pressed against Azil's hole while bobbing down a little further. He felt the head of Azil's cock pop into his throat. There was a second of panic over not being able to breathe, but then Solomon firmly reminded himself that he could always lean away.

Instead, he swallowed, and Azil jolted under him like he'd been hit with a live wire.

Spunk jetted into Solomon's throat. He pulled back and caught the next shot on his tongue.

Azil shouted, the sound raw and broken. He squirmed and panted until his cock stopped dribbling out cum.

"Oh my gods," he repeated a few times.

Solomon rubbed over Azil's pucker and licked his balls.

Azil pulled Solomon's hips down and sucked his dick right into the warm cavern of his mouth. He went after Solomon with an eagerness he'd not shown earlier. Not that he'd been complacent.

But now, it was quite clear that Azil was determined to drive Solomon insane with want.

It didn't take long. Azil sucked him in deep, no more timid licks and suckling. He also pressed that dry finger further into Solomon's ass.

The burn was slight. The pleasure was great. Solomon saw stars as he rutted back and forth between that digit and Azil's mouth.

When he was able to sink into Azil's throat, and Azil pressed a second finger into him, Solomon broke. He threw his head back, his orgasm so intense the shout clogged in his throat. Solomon couldn't do anything but feel as he came, his ass and cock in sync, bliss swirling back and forth from them both.

He didn't know how long it lasted. Eventually he became aware of the fact that his hole was empty and his dick no longer in that wonderfully wet embrace. He was also on his back, with Azil lying halfway on him.

It was good. Even despite Solomon's worry, this moment was good, and peaceful. He let himself rest for a little while. The problems he faced weren't going away. They'd still be there when he woke up, but for now, he wanted just that one blip in time where he was lying, content, with his mate.

# Chapter Seven

"Remus said they went south," Steven argued. "Why are you being a jerk about us going after them?"

Bobby stepped right up to Steven and growled. "Because he also said we needed to stay here. You need to stop forgettin' that little bit of information. You either trust our shaman, or you don't." Bobby let some of that power he held in roll off him. "I get that you're worried about Solomon, but Remus says we stay, then we stay, because maybe somethin' worse will happen if we don't. He couldn't see clearly. That doesn't happen to him often, and it worries me that he can't see it. It damn sure ought to worry you, too."

"Just because there was no trace of anyone snooping around the house doesn't mean it isn't being watched from a distance," Sully added. "Something very wrong is going on. Even I can feel it now."

Steven could, too, and it was driving him up the wall to be so helpless. "I can't just sit here."

"You ain't just sittin' here. You have a whole herd of kids that need takin' care of," Bobby said. "Do that. You think Solomon would want 'em all left with us?

He never did let 'em hang around the pack often. Think about that, dumbass."

Steven snarled and before he knew what he was doing, he had a fist raised.

Bobby grinned. "Bring it on, bitch, if it'll make you feel better. I'll even keep my alpha mojo locked up so I can whoop your ass fair and square."

"Steven…" Shaun began.

"Let him," Cole said quietly. "They both need to get this over with. It's been coming for years."

Steven lowered his hand and took a fighting stance, feet shoulder width apart, body loose but ready to spring.

"No hard feelin's, right?" Bobby asked.

"None at all," Steven agreed. He needed to thump something before he lost his mind.

"What's happening here?" Adal asked, charging into the room.

Cole held up a hand to stop Adal from interfering. "It's okay. Let them do this once and for all."

Adal took a step forward. "But—"

Dorso hooked an arm around Adal's middle and pulled him back. "Listen to Cole, honey."

Adal bit his lip but nodded.

Steven gave him an approving look then focused on his opponent. It wasn't that he hated Bobby. They did tend to butt heads from time to time, and a good old-fashioned fight was what they both needed to clear the air between them. Steven couldn't completely follow a man he could defeat. He knew that about himself. "You can use your alpha mojo if you need to," he offered.

Bobby laughed at him.

"He won't need to," Sully said.

Steven watched his opponent. Bobby was just standing there, not even trying to position himself for a fight. It pissed Steven off that the asshole wasn't even the slightest bit concerned "I'm serious about this."

Bobby arched that eyebrow, the one that almost met his hairline when he did that. "I'm aware. You're too serious, Steven. That's always a mistake."

Steven's blood did a slow simmer as anger coursed through his veins. "And being a joker all the time is just fool—"

He didn't get any further before Bobby was on him. The alpha moved so fast, to say he was a blur was an understatement.

Steven threw up his fists, trying to protect his face. The solid kick to his ribs sent him reeling. It also knocked the breath out of him and possibly made his heart stop for a second until it restarted when he hit the wall.

"Shit!" someone exclaimed. "That's not playing around!"

"No playing here," Cole said. "Bobby doesn't play like this."

*Shit, whose side is Cole on?*

*"Yours, babe, but you're going to get your ass handed to you in a matter of seconds,"* Cole thought to him.

Steven tried to stand upright but Bobby was everywhere, and he wasn't pulling any punches. He landed several to Steven's torso and back. Steven hunched over, trying to keep his head and neck covered.

Bobby kicked at his ankles.

Steven flailed, swinging blindly. He managed to hit Bobby hard enough that his hand ached, but Bobby, the crazy fucker, just laughed and took Steven down with a much more powerful kick.

Steven hit the floor hard. He didn't give up. He bucked and hit, kicked and even bit.

Bobby cackled and bit him back, bringing up blood. When Bobby grabbed him by the hair and smacked Steven's head against the floor, Steven saw stars.

"Ready to behave?" Bobby asked, only mildly out of breath. "You feelin' that respect yet?"

Steven thought about it. He could probably keep on fighting, but why? Bobby had him down and was showing every sign of being the more powerful of them both. "Yeah," Steven got out.

Bobby groaned and flopped to the side, onto his ass. "Thank fuck. I'm gettin' too old to be teachin' smart-asses who's the boss."

Steven sat up and rubbed the back of his head. He had a knot there, but he likely had knots all over. He'd had his ass handed to him in a matter of minutes by a whirlwind of crazy.

*"And powerful. That's what you needed,"* Cole thought. Out loud, he said, "Shaun went to get some ice."

Bobby got up and offered Steven a hand. "Now, are we done?"

Steven nodded. "Yeah, we are."

"Good. I needed a fight with someone I could trust." Bobby popped his back then his knuckles. "We should spar on a regular basis. I promise not to go gentle on you."

The offer was a balm to Steven's pride. "I don't think I'll be much of a challenge."

Bobby grinned. "I'll teach you a few things."

"Now that Adal's here, he could stay with the kids," Steven pressed.

"Shoulda known you weren't gonna shut up," Bobby groused. "And the answer is still no. No offense, Adal, but you aren't as ornery as Steven. He needs to guard the kids."

"I agree," Adal said. "Steven, you look, um, like you might be sore in the morning."

"Or for a few days," Dorso chimed in, smiling happily. "If I mention karma, are you going to growl?"

"I should have punched you harder," Steven informed Dorso, but in reality, he liked his brother-in-law. Dorso was very good to Adal.

"What's happening now?" Adal asked.

"Nothing," Steven answered angrily. "Remus says Solomon will be back, but he doesn't know how or when."

"Soon, that's what he said," Cole added. "I think he's even going to call Rolly back from his spiritual retreat."

"Been 'spiritually retreating' for almost five years with just short visits home now and then, so it's about damn time," Bobby grumbled. "I miss that asshole."

Steven didn't really know Rolly, so he didn't care one way or another that Remus' oldest son had been off somewhere meditating or whatever for years now. Except that it mattered to Cole, so in that respect, Steven hoped Rolly came home soon. Cole missed him, too.

"Is there imminent danger?" Adal asked, his expression steeped in concern. "Why would he need to call Rolly in?"

Why hadn't Steven wondered that himself? *Because I was too busy being pissed off over not being allowed to go after Solomon. But if Rolly's being called back, then…*

"Probably 'cuz things are about to go to shit around here," Bobby said slowly, as if he weren't concerned at all.

Steven knew better. Bobby put his pack first, and protected them fiercely. Whoever had taken Solomon would be lucky if Steven got to them before Bobby did. Maybe. Steven would try not to give in to the urge to torture them before killing them.

A strange, cold current washed over him. Steven flinched at the discomforting sensation. No one else seemed to be affected by it, or so he thought until his mates reached out to him mentally.

*"What in the hells was that?"* Shaun was the first to ask.

*"Evil,"* Cole supplied. *"Unadulterated evil. Someone is sending very bad magic our way."*

*"Another shaman. God damn it!"* Shaun was not only angry, but scared as well.

*"We need to go talk to Remus, now."* Steven ignored his aches and pains. He held out a hand to Bobby. "We need to go."

Bobby shook it. "Do you, now? Hmm. You gonna tell me what's goin' on?"

Steven looked from Bobby to Adal. "I don't know, but it's not good, and we need to talk to Remus about it. Adal, if you and Dorso will go to the house? There are guards there, waiting for you."

"You'll tell me what's happening?" Adal asked.

"Of course." Steven watched his brother leave.

Bobby cleared his throat. "You don't have to tell me. You can bet your ass I'm going with you to talk to Remus."

Steven sighed. He didn't even bother arguing about it.

* * * *

"We need to find a vehicle and get back sooner," Solomon said. "Crossing the border will be a problem."

"No it won't," Azil was happy to tell him. "We have a tunnel. We can d-drive to it then steal a car once we're across."

"And steal a car to get there?" Solomon asked. "I tell the kids—"

"Would you rather walk?" Leeloo snapped. "Even in shifted form, it will take us days to get you home. I can't run as fast as you, either. I'm tiring too quickly now."

Azil was worried about Leeloo. In a day's time, she seemed to have grown more thin and drawn. She had dark circles under her eyes.

"I hate the Vento clan, and yet I want to go back," she said. "Must be missing Luto."

Considering that Leeloo had been sent out on assignments before, Azil thought that a strange statement.

"There's a city up ahead, about five miles," Leeloo continued. "I'll find a vehicle there. Tell your conscience to deal with it, Solomon, because it's going to happen."

Solomon didn't look happy about it, but he didn't argue.

"In fact, you both stay here. Do...whatever, and I'll be back with food, clothes and transportation." Leeloo didn't wait for an answer.

Solomon pulled Azil over into the shade. "Tell me about your life. Do you have family? What was it like growing up in the clan?"

Azil didn't want to talk about himself. He wanted Solomon, wanted them to speak with their bodies in the most basic and stirring of ways.

Solomon cupped his chin and Azil had to take a deep breath before he looked him in the eyes.

"I want to know what kind of hold that clan has on you, the way they brainwashed you. I have over a dozen brothers and sisters I'm raising. They're all very strong-willed."

Azil couldn't feel Solomon mentally, didn't know where he was going with what he was saying.

Solomon leaned in for a soft kiss before he spoke again. "They might scare you, or take advantage. None of them are bad, they're just kids, sometimes whining, arguing, but most of the time good, loving. Doesn't mean they wouldn't try to walk all over you."

"Oh." Azil thought he had it figured out. "You think I'm not strong enough for them?"

"Are you?" Solomon asked. "No, let me rephrase that. Do *you* think you're strong enough? You'll be my partner. I'm sorry if it comes as a shock, because you're getting a great big family and a lot of responsibility out of the blue."

Azil wanted it, all of it. "I want to be free," he whispered, hoping Solomon understood.

"From the way you've been told things should be," Solomon accurately surmised.

"Yes." Azil ached for that. "I was raised up with the other males. We weren't kept by our families. Only the female children are kept by the women, by their mothers. The boys, they are put in one place and are watched over, but not raised like the girls. We were told that males are weaker, unable to control our bodies' urges, to think past our hormones. Past our genitals. Men are violent, and unfaithful, incapable of commitment or intelligence at the level of females."

Solomon let go of Azil's chin. "Are all the clans in your area like that?"

"I don't think so," Azil answered, wishing Solomon would touch him again. "Leeloo said hers wasn't. Our clan, it wasn't always that way. I heard from one male, who'd found favoritism with his owner, that our clan wasn't even an old on. What we'd been taught was lies to keep us under control. He was... He was nice. He taught me to read a little, and to write, before his owner traded him to someone else."

"You understand, then, that women aren't evil, no more so than men," Solomon pointed out. "There are men who do the same, only to women. It's the person, not the gender, that makes a person good or bad."

"I know that here—" Azil tapped his temple. "Inside, too, I still think I'm supposed to be less. I don't think that will change any time soon."

Solomon sat and stretched his legs out. "Come here."

Azil moved closer. "There?"

"On my lap." Solomon patted his thighs. "Put your butt right here."

There was a growing bulge very close to where Solomon had touched.

Azil sat clumsily, feeling like a fool. "Sorry."

"Don't be." Solomon helped get him settled, turning Azil until he was actually straddling Solomon's lap. "There. Now, here's the thing. I would imagine it'd take time to undo years of brainwashing. How old are you?"

"Somewhere around nineteen. A couple of months past that," Azil clarified. "Old for an unkept man, but no one wants me."

"Old?" Solomon clicked his tongue. "Please, I'm twenty-two, as close as we can figure. I've never even kissed someone in a passionate way until yesterday, when I kissed you. As for no one wanting you, I very obviously do." Solomon rubbed his hardening erection against Azil's bottom. "Very much."

"Then you could take me?" Azil asked, the idea of it thrilling him. "I've seen it done many times with nothing at all—"

"Which would hurt you," Solomon cut in with. "Absolutely not. I heal very fast, so we could do it the other way if it would make you feel better about us, but I'd prefer to wait until we had the proper lubricant on hand."

"Make me feel better?" Azil didn't like the sound of that. "Like you'd fuck me for my own sake?"

Solomon burst out laughing.

Azil started to get up, but Solomon held onto him, locking his arms around Azil.

"Oh no, I'm not laughing at you, but at the idea that I wouldn't love to lay you out and make love to you." Solomon kissed him then—a hard, fast, claiming kiss. "I want you, bad enough to know I won't be able to be gentle when I finally get to have you. The least I can do is hold off until we have lube."

"Spit—" Azil began.

"No," Solomon said firmly. Then before Azil could argue any further, Solomon fisted Azil's cock. "No, not for that. For this, yes." Solomon eased Azil back onto the ground. He took Azil's shaft into his mouth and sucked.

Azil arched, his eyes rolling wildly as pleasure suffused him. It didn't take long at all for his balls to draw tight. Solomon only had to take him in a few times. Azil cried out as he came, and he whimpered with each successive spurt of cum.

When he was coming back down from his release, Solomon licked him tenderly then left off stimulating his cock.

Azil was barely cognizant of Solomon kneeling over him and quickly jacking off. He pumped his load onto Azil's chest, which brought Azil to full attention again. Azil ran his fingers through a splotch of spunk then licked Solomon's seed off them.

"Gods," Solomon huffed. "Do that again."

Azil did, then again, and he kept at it until he'd cleaned up all the cum from his chest.

Solomon watched him with something much like awe the entire time. "So sexy," Solomon finally said. He took a kiss, a long, thorough one that had Azil's dick half-hard by the time it ended.

Still, neither he nor Solomon pressed for anything more than a long, sweet make-out session. Kisses, soft touches — Azil happily passed the time with Solomon while waiting for Leeloo to return.

Eventually, desire built up between them again in gradual degrees. Even so, Azil didn't push for more. There was something good and right to what they were doing, then it became more intense, with need rolling into Azil, making him want more.

Had Leeloo not pulled up in a rusted-out car then, Azil might have gotten up the nerve to again try to persuade Solomon to fuck him. No, not fuck him. *Make love.* Azil liked the sound of that, as if the act itself would be tender and full of meaning instead of just a show of dominance.

There would be nothing false or cruel about Solomon touching him. It wouldn't be a contest of wills, or a war of egos. Azil was beginning to understand what being mates truly meant. His instincts, buried under a lifetime of counter-training, were surfacing and easing his way with his mate.

And Leeloo, she was showing him moment by moment that women weren't all like the ones he'd known.

"You have sisters?" he found himself asking Solomon after they'd gotten dressed and loaded into the car.

"Several," Solomon told him.

"I'm going to nap in the back seat," Leeloo informed them. "Eat whatever food you want. There is water also. Bottled."

Solomon took the bottle of water Azil handed him. "Thanks. One of my brothers, he might—well, I think he's, uh…"

Azil was confused. "You think he's what?"

"Gay isn't a problem for you, obviously," Solomon said, steering the car onto the road.

"No, obviously it isn't, but it is for my clan. It isn't something that was allowed," Azil mused. "Some of the boys, when we could get away with it, we would do things, but I thought all boys did. We didn't want to get caught, either, because we knew we'd be beaten for it. Which still didn't stop us."

"Kids are curious," Solomon agreed. "I have a brother, Erdwin, he's just turned eighteen. I believe he feels he was born in the wrong body. I hope he's comfortable enough to talk to me about it. I've seen some of the clothes he has tried to hide."

"I don't understand what you mean." Azil wasn't stupid but he still couldn't grasp what Solomon was trying to say.

"Erdwin has the male parts, but feels like a female, like his soul was put in the wrong body before he was born," Solomon explained. "He's dropped hints to me, but hasn't come out and said so. Will that be a problem for you, if he dresses and acts how he feels he should?"

Azil examined the question thoroughly, and his own reaction to it. "I don't understand why it would be my problem." He wanted all of Solomon's family to like him. "I have a lot to learn, I know that, but I don't think I'm a judgmental person."

"The damage hasn't been done to him that it has to many of the males in the clan," Leeloo added from her back seat bed. "Azil is a good soul. There are few enough of them around. Even in the clan I was born into, evil was pervasive, but we didn't enslave entire genders."

"I thought you were going to sleep," Solomon teased.

"I am." Leeloo didn't speak again.

Azil and Solomon chatted, getting to know each other. Azil didn't think he was an interesting man, but Solomon seemed to hang on his every word.

Solomon talked a little about his childhood, enough for Azil to learn that it was much more horrific than his.

"Does it make me a bad person to say I'm glad your father is dead?" he asked of Solomon.

"I'm thrilled he's dead," Solomon said bluntly. "He wasn't a father in any sense of the word. He was a sadistic man who wanted to rape and kill. And he did."

Azil couldn't quite repress a shudder. "It's wrong to force anyone to have sex."

"It is," Solomon agreed. "I wish I knew whether my mother was a good person, what she was like. I hope that she wasn't like him in any way. I'd like to know I have the blood of one decent person in me."

"You might learn more about her through the Vento clan, if…if the queen is defeated," Azil said. He plucked at the piece of chicken he'd pulled out to eat. "Do you want some?"

"Please," Solomon told him. "As for the queen and defeating her, that's not my place, my calling, however you want to put it. I need to get back to my family. I have to be there with them. I've always protected them, Azil, and to be taken from them hurts in a way I can't explain."

"I'm sorry." Azil truly was. He'd played a part in hurting Solomon.

"Don't blame yourself. You didn't know, and if you hadn't come along to help them kidnap me, we'd never have met. That would totally suck." Solomon winked at him.

Azil choked on the bite of chicken he'd just tried to swallow.

Solomon reached over and patted him on the back. "You okay?"

Azil got the food down. "You winked."

Solomon chuckled. "I won't do it again if you're going to keel over from it."

"You have such interesting eyes." Oh now, now Azil was just blurting out thoughts…thoughtlessly.

"Interesting," Solomon repeated. "Is that bad or good? I know I look different, unlike anyone I've seen, at least. My shifted form coloring is odd, too. A leopard-jaguar with no rosettes at all, just white tips here and there. My odd eyes, my striped hair—"

"But I like all of those things," Azil dared to interrupt. "I do. They're interesting and, well, pretty. I would say pretty, unless that offends you."

"Why would it?" Solomon was beaming at him. "Nothing wrong with the word pretty, or its meaning. I'm a big guy, I'm secure. You can call me anything you want to."

That eased some of Azil's concerns. "Oh, okay. Was it hard for you, looking different? It was for me. Not being able to tan, having freckles, this hair and my eyes. My parents were, by all accounts, normal looking. No one knows why I came out looking like a freak."

"You don't look like a freak. Probably, there are recessive genes somewhere or something like that. I'm not great at biology or genetics. Haven't had a lot of education up until I was rescued." Solomon turned on the headlights. "You speak two languages?"

"English and Portuguese," Azil said. "We are educated about certain things, so we can hold a decent conversation with whoever takes us. Not as educated as I wanted to be."

"You can take online classes and there are endless things to learn about that way. My oldest sisters, Elena and Kylie, they're both taking online college courses." Solomon frowned then. "Elena is one of my full-blooded siblings. The other two are guys, Jerek and Keno. They build computers and sell them. Two techie-smarties, those guys. They're twins, and lucky to have survived. I'm two years older than Elena. She's twenty. The twins are seventeen. Bashuan kept my mother locked away for his own sick reasons for many years. I only found out after she was dead." He shook his head. "That's not the point. I'm explaining about the family. After Elena, there's a year gap before the four sibs that just turned eighteen, all of whom have different moms. It can get crazy in our house."

"It sounds like fun, actually." Azil asked, "How old is the youngest?"

"Eight, and she's definitely testing her boundaries. They all seem to go through that stage." Solomon continued talking about his family for a long while after that.

Azil began to hope that he could fit in. He wanted to belong.

# Chapter Eight

Solomon parked the car. It was dark out, no moon in sight. That was a good thing.

Leeloo groaned and stumbled as she got out of the vehicle. "I don't think I can make it. I need... I need to go back."

"Need to?" Solomon asked, squatting beside her. He ran his hands over her, looking for injuries. "Where do you hurt?"

"Everywhere, inside. In my soul," she rasped. "I have to go back."

"Have to..." An idea popped into his head. "Like a compulsion? A true need?"

When she nodded, he felt that he had the answer.

"Who is he?"

Leeloo scowled at him. "Who is he, who? I told you about my brother."

"But you've left him behind before," Azil added.

"Another man, then. One you want," Solomon stressed.

"I want no man. I told you that before." Leeloo sat up. "No man."

"Ah." Solomon rocked back on his heels, nearly toppling over onto his butt. "She, then. A woman you want. Your mate, I'd bet."

"No, it can't—" Leeloo started hyperventilating.

"Mates do exist, you've seen me and Azil," Solomon continued. "You said before that you wanted to go back but didn't know why. Yet you've left before, so it must be someone you only just encountered. Who is your mate, Leeloo?"

"Gods, gods," she croaked. "I didn't know. I— The same laws stand for women as for men. No same-sex relationships. The clan needs to grow bigger, stronger, and that means as many children as possible. She won't want me. She will hate me for this."

Solomon knew better than that. "She won't. She's your mate, and right now, she is probably every bit as confused and ill as you are. That can happen with mates, I've heard. Being apart is physically painful. I didn't know it could get this bad." For all of his knowledge on the matter, it didn't usually get so bad. He'd never heard of mates being apart for long at all and had nothing to judge by. "Go back. Sneak into the clan if you have to."

"I will, because we killed the other guards, and I'm letting you go." Leeloo got up and dusted herself off. "Or I could lie."

"Tell your queen that we escaped, and killed everyone except you." Solomon looked at Azil. "It might be better if she believes you're dead."

"I like the idea of being a bad guy to her, though," Azil protested.

Solomon considered that for a moment. "But would she use that as an excuse to come down harder on the men in the clan?"

"Very likely," Leeloo answered first. "So you're no longer of this world, Azil. You died valiantly, though. I'll make sure she knows how you led the guards when Balani was torn to shreds."

"Good luck, Leeloo. I suspect that my brother Steven will be coming to pay a visit to your queen in the very near future." Solomon would try to talk him out of it, but Steven would want retribution.

"I look forward to that day." Leeloo tossed them the bag that still had a small reserve of food and water in it. "Take this. I have no guilt when it comes to surviving. You seem to, though."

Solomon caught the bag then handed it to Azil. "I don't like the idea of stealing, but we're sure not going to walk the next three hundred or so miles."

"We can find a phone once we're across the border. Well, I think it's about ten miles or so to the closest home, but after that, you could call and let your family know you're okay?" Azil suggested.

"And that I've found my mate," Solomon added. "Yes. Let's go. I want to go home."

The tunnel was crudely dug but effective. It started over a quarter mile from the border, and ran almost half a mile through to the other side. Parts of it were very unstable. Solomon discovered that he'd become a tad claustrophobic in the past few years.

And that he really didn't want to die by being buried alive.

"It's more stable than it looks," Azil assured him. "There are support beams."

Solomon just hurried through the underground hell as fast as he could. He'd have shifted but they'd need the clothes Leeloo had brought them.

He exited the tunnel and came out through a rotting shed. Solomon paused to listen for anyone outside and heard only crickets and cicadas. He smelled nothing unusual, save the faint odor of Azil and the guards from their previous entrance into the States.

Azil pressed up against him. Tentatively at first, then with more confidence, sliding his arms around Solomon's waist.

"I'm a little nervous, but I'm glad you'll be home soon."

"We," Solomon corrected. "We'll be home soon."

"Okay." Azil released him. "We can jog, if you're up for it."

Solomon smirked at the challenge. "Winner gets a blow job."

He got a head start while Azil gawped at him.

Honestly, Azil couldn't see any way of losing. He'd either get to push into the silky heat of Solomon's mouth, or suck on that big cock of Solomon's, drive him past all control. Azil watched Solomon run, the way his taut buttocks flexed, the long, clean strides he took.

Had anyone ever told him he'd be...happy, he'd have called them a liar. At least in his head. Not out loud, because he didn't like confrontations. No—he'd never been allowed to have a confrontation. Arguing got a man whipped until his back was a mass of raw meat. Azil had been quiet most of his life.

He didn't even know who he really was.

*"Yes, you do. You're a good man, with a strong heart, a quick mind, and a gorgeous cock."*

Solomon's thoughts startled Azil into action. He took off, letting his body go, running for the sheer enjoyment of playing with his mate.

His mate. It would take a long time for Azil to get beyond his shock at that. Strange how everything inside him was waking up now. Solomon had done that for him, bringing Azil into the world that existed outside the oppressive clan.

Each bounding step he took brought a greater sense of freedom to Azil. He was smiling like a lunatic, laughing even on occasion, within five minutes.

Solomon turned and ran backwards, grinning goofily at him. The sensations between them flowed easily, generously, through the mental link they shared.

Azil didn't want to wait until they reached civilization to touch Solomon. He wanted to pounce on the man right there, amidst the nothingness that surrounded them.

Solomon stopped running. "Azil," he murmured.

Azil slowed down.

But Solomon had said they needed lube. There would be none of the kind of taking Azil was craving.

He sprinted past Solomon.

"You—" Solomon barked out a laugh. "You turkey!"

Azil surprised himself by squealing with laughter when Solomon tackled him. They didn't fall hard since they skidded first, and Solomon rolled them to a gentle enough halt.

"I've got you now," Solomon growled before kissing him soundly.

"I want... I want..." Azil groaned in frustration. It shouldn't be so hard to voice his desires. Wouldn't be, if he hadn't been raised up to believe that his desires were wrong.

"You can have it. I can handle it—"

Azil bucked. "No, that isn't— I want you, in me. To make love to me," he finished in a bare wisp of sound.

Solomon sealed his mouth over Azil's. He pushed his tongue in deep, laying claim.

Azil loved it, writhing and clinging and whimpering as he was taken. He wanted the same thing, with no clothes in the way, and a damned vat of lube since Solomon was so set on having the stuff.

"A vat?" Solomon asked, his breath wafting over Azil's chin. "A vat would do for a start. We're young. We have many, many years of sex in front of us. We'll need dozens of vats." Then he pursed his lips. "How big is a vat anyway? We may need a more specific weight or measurement here. Like fifty-five gallon drums."

Azil giggled, a sound he'd not made since his childhood, before he'd had the seriousness of life drilled into him.

"That's adorable," Solomon said before kissing him again. "And we need to go. Get your sexy butt up."

Solomon stood and pulled Azil to his feet. "You really are stacked, Azil. Look at all these muscles. I bet you could take me in a fight."

Azil held up his hands. "I wouldn't. I can't fight you."

"I know. I meant if we weren't mates. You're very strong." Solomon nuzzled his cheek.

"You are, too," Azil said. Solomon had shoulders almost as broad as Azil's.

Solomon nipped his neck. "I want to mark you again, and I want you to do it to me, too." He moved back. "Is the race still on? I can't decide if I want to win or lose."

Azil had thought the very same thing himself. "We could do what we did before."

"Sixty-nine, yeah." Solomon popped Azil on the butt then took off.

Azil didn't stand there staring like a goofball this time. He kept up with Solomon.

The first building they approached was abandoned, but the second was an actual home. It seemed the people in it were asleep. Solomon said he didn't think waking them was a good idea as it could get them shot.

Azil agreed that moving on was wise.

"This place is open." Solomon pointed to a gas station. "Maybe I can get someone to let me make a call on their cellphone." Then he whooped. "Oh my gods! Is that a pay phone? It is!"

Azil assumed Solomon was talking about the thing on the post a dozen feet from the gas station itself. "There's a phone there?"

"Yes. I've seen them on TV and in a few places around San Antonio. Didn't think I'd get this lucky. Come on." He took Azil by the elbow and jogged to the phone.

Azil watched, fascinated, as Solomon got someone on the phone and succeeded in making a call.

Solomon talked in a quick, excited manner as he explained to someone where he was.

"How are all the kids? That's great. Good, give them my love. I'm with my mate now. Yes, with my mate. Mate. Mate! I'll explain the rest later. Just, come get us. Thanks." Solomon hung up. "That was my other older brother, Adal. He squealed so loud when I mentioned you that my ear is still ringing. Do you want a drink?"

Azil inhaled sharply. "The bag. I must have dropped it in the tunnel." He'd been worried about Solomon, and thinking he might have to carry the man again.

"It's okay. Leeloo stuffed a few dollars in my pants pocket when she gave them to me. We can get a soda or some water." Solomon waited.

"Okay," Azil said.

But it wasn't water or soda that caught his eye. Azil saw the lubricant behind the counter.

Solomon hissed under his breath. "No."

Azil didn't try to hide his disappointment.

Solomon paid for their waters.

Outside, he explained to Azil why he'd said no. "The lube was too expensive, and there is nowhere we could use it, if you know what I mean. We can't even collect on our winnings around here." His pupils expanded. "And I want to be somewhere alone with you, where I can strip you down and learn every secret your body wants to tell me when I make love to you."

"Oh. Oh." Azil struggled to get words out. "I want that, too."

Solomon took him by the elbow again. "Then we wait. We walk, and we talk, and we sit at the diner where Steven will be picking us up in a few hours. Probably less. I have a feeling he'll be driving as fast as he can to get here."

The diner was of the twenty-four hour variety, and common in the South, according to Solomon.

Azil didn't like the burnt grease odor of the place. He picked at his pancakes. They were good, and a new food to him, but the syrup was too sweet, and anyway, Azil was so nervous that eating wasn't really working for him.

Less than an hour after they'd sat down, a big, scary man walked into the diner. Two men flanked him. His steely gaze went right to Azil.

Azil tried not to quake in his seat.

"Steven! You're early," Solomon said as he stood up. "Ah, the jet?"

Steven was exuding enough anger and power that Azil wanted to crawl on his belly—to the back door and run.

"Stop it."

Azil wasn't certain who Solomon was talking to at first.

Then Solomon clarified it. "Seriously, Steven. Cut it out. Cole, Shaun, control your idiot."

"His scent is familiar," Steven rumbled. Then he cracked his knuckles.

For some reason, that was the thing that struck Azil as ridiculous. He tipped his chin up and got out of his seat. Gritting his teeth, Azil didn't speak, but he glared back as fiercely as he could.

"How about I pay the bill and we leave?" one of the other two men said.

"Good. You do that, Shaun." Solomon rested a hand on the small of Azil's back. "The rest of us will wait outside."

Azil kept his head up as he walked past Steven. He wasn't going to cower. He was free now, and that wasn't going to be taken away from him.

Outside, Steven paced but didn't speak.

"I'm Cole," the third man said, offering Azil his hand.

"Remus' son," Azil murmured. "I'm Azil, from the Vento jaguar clan."

"You're Solomon's mate," Cole clarified. "That's obvious. I can see that the two of you are bonded somewhat already."

"I didn't know it was possible. The clan, it's... It's wrong," Azil finished lamely.

Cole nodded as he gestured at Steven. "Stop, okay? Let's hear him out."

Steven hung his head for a moment then inhaled slowly. He exhaled and looked at Azil. "I'm listening."

Solomon muttered and moved over to give Steven a hug. "I'm here, and unharmed. I learned more about my past. And he's my *mate*, Steven. You know what that means."

Steven didn't look pleased. "I do. What's your name?"

Azil was certain Steven had heard him, but let it go. "Azil."

"And what did you tell Cole?" Steven prodded.

Azil wished he didn't blush so easily. He started explaining about the clan, the way men were treated, the secrets Leeloo had shared about Wyanem betraying Irial. Shaun got to hear almost all of it as well. The men stood in the parking lot, listening to Azil's recounting of his life and what he knew of the clan.

"It's not an old clan," he finished with. "We're lied to about many things, but when there is no one else to counter those lies, what else do we have to believe?"

"Where's this curandera?" Steven asked. "How powerful is she?"

"Leeloo said the curandera Tritaya was coming here. Or to the pack you live with, rather. As far as I know, she's the most powerful curandera there is, but..." Azil shrugged. "I don't know very much."

"You know more about this than we do." Steven pointed to a big black vehicle with rental plates. "Get in that. We got the jet here, but we're driving back. The pilot said the plane needed a few things done to it before he took off in it again. Plus I hate flying."

Azil thought it might be cool to be up in the clouds or above them.

*Or it might be terrifying. Falling, that would be bad.*

"We need to get a hold of Remus, let him know there's a loony curandera lurking around somewhere. Cole, can you call your dad?" Steven asked.

"Sure I can. Will he hear the phone, that's another question entirely. He was doing several ceremonies to reach out to Rolly." Cole took out a cell phone and began messing with it. "Cliff's probably assisting him, too, but there's always Bobby if all else fails."

"Bobby is going to want to tear that clan apart," Steven informed everyone. "I'll be helping him."

"Where you go we go, and all that romantic shit," Shaun said. "And no, I don't have to do the laundry. We aren't at the house with the kids, so I can cuss like a grown up."

"I'm an adult and I don't cuss," Solomon pointed out.

Azil replayed every moment he'd spent with Solomon. The man really didn't curse.

"That's because, up until these shenanigans started, you were *always* at the house," Steven retorted. "And by the way, Vanda was afraid she'd scared you off. What's up with that?"

Azil wondered the same thing. "Who's Vanda?" He didn't remember Solomon mentioning any sisters by that name.

Solomon's cheeks turned ruddy. "A wolf shifter. She asked if I was interested in messing around once, and I told her no. When she tried to talk to me after that, I thought she was still trying to get me to date her or whatever. I might have overreacted, and she might have gotten angry about it."

"Might have?" Steven asked, looking in the rearview mirror.

"Fine. Did." Solomon leaned his head against the back of the seat. "And I'm done with that discussion."

Azil watched him sleep for the rest of the drive, relieved that the other three men left him alone.

There were several people gathered by where Steven parked the vehicle. Two of them, an older man with stark white hair, and the dark-headed guy beside him, exuded enough power that Azil knew who they were.

Remus would be the one with white hair, and the darker man was Cliff, Remus' mate.

Azil had no trouble picking out the alpha, either. Bobby had a laid-back look that was quite deceitful. There was a strength in him any shifter with an iota of sense could detect.

Between those three powerful men, Azil didn't believe the curandera stood a chance. He'd been around her before, and she didn't feel nearly as threatening as Remus, Cliff and Bobby.

"We're home?" Solomon asked, his voice slurred from sleep.

"We are," Shaun said. "Azil, I hope you'll be comfortable here. Eventually. You might be weirded out first, because of all the changes, and — "

Cole nudged Shaun hard. "Shaun, stop."

Solomon snickered and linked a hand with Azil's. "Ready for this?"

*No.* "Yes." Azil got out with Solomon right behind him.

Bobby started forward, but Remus held a hand up. "No. No posturing and bullshit with him. Welcome, Azil."

Azil felt that welcome all the way into his bones.

Remus smiled and opened his arms.

Azil was confused until Solomon gave him a gentle push. "He's offering you a blessing."

Azil needed every blessing he could get. He was touched by Remus' generosity.

Then he was actually touched by the shaman himself as Remus hugged him.

Words Azil didn't recognize spilled from Remus' lips. Unfamiliar as they were, Azil was still comforted. He closed his eyes and imagined he could see each word taking shape around him, swirling with the others Remus spoke until Azil was ensconced in a safe net formed by those letters.

Remus touched his forehead to Azil's, and warmth flowed from the shaman into Azil.

When Remus let him go, Azil felt rejuvenated and boneless at the same time. "Thank you," he found the voice to say.

Then he was looking at Cliff. It was disconcerting to see Cliff staring back at him with two different colored eyes. One was silver, the other gold.

Cliff gave him a cocky grin. "I'm not going to bite."

"Cliff," Remus admonished. "Azil, don't let him get to you. Cliff overcompensates at times."

"I— What?" Cliff snapped. "I don't need to compensate for anything. I have a big—"

"Not to be confused with you *are* a big dick," Bobby said as he flapped a hand their way. "That's what Remus was referrin' to. You overcompensate for being a great big dick."

Azil glanced from Cliff to the alpha. "It's like being back in the room with the teenage boys again," he said unthinkingly. "All bravado and bragging, chest-thumping and measuring—er..."

Cliff nodded. "We could do that. Someone got a tape measure?"

"Y'all are insane," Shaun said. "Grow up, people."

"You're talkin' to your alpha like that?" Bobby asked lazily.

Shaun turned his nose up. "I'm talking to an immature doofus— Two of 'em, actually. Alpha"—he pointed at Bobby, then at Cliff—"father-in-law, whatever. Neither of you are acting your age, that's for sure."

"It's no fun to act my age." Cliff poked Shaun's chest. "I'd rather act your IQ points. Twelve."

"Someone's feeling their oats, aren't they?" Cole asked. "Dad, you need to control your monkey."

"My monkey?" Remus looked Cliff up and down. "He's mine, and he can shift into two different beasts, neither of which is a monkey."

Azil knew he was staring, but he couldn't believe his ears.

Cliff buffed his fingernails on his shirt. "Yup. I'm that kinda special. If I *could* shift into a monkey, I'd be sure to fling my shit at you, Bob."

"Bob?" Bobby pressed his lips tightly together.

"Bobby, don't let him provoke you," another man said. Bobby's mate would be Azil's guess.

"Nah, I kinda like it," Bobby said, then he laughed. "Yeah, you can call me Bob, you dumbass."

"Bob you dumbass is a real mouthful," Cliff drawled. "Let's just go with dumbass."

"If I hadn't just bruised my fists whaling on Steven earlier, I'd take you out, Cliff. Later, man. It's a date," Bobby promised.

Azil moved to stand beside Solomon. "Are they always so…violent?"

"They're joking, for the most part," Solomon said. "Except, Bobby? Steven? What's that about Bobby whaling on you?"

Steven hitched one shoulder up in a shrug. "Tension release."

"So, Azil." Bobby strolled over and stopped in front of him. "I'm gonna take it that you won't be doin' any more stupid shit. You come back with me and tell me what the hell you were doin' takin' Solomon away from his family. And you" — Bobby pointed at Solomon — "you don't argue about it. This is my pack, and you're a part of it. I'm keepin' you safe and I need insider information about this clan I'm gonna tear apart."

# Chapter Nine

Solomon didn't try to run interference for Azil with Bobby. Bobby was a fair alpha. Solomon did wonder what had gone down between Steven and Bobby. Whatever it was, the two men seemed to be friendlier than they had been before.

It wasn't just Bobby that Azil talked to. Inside the large office sat Remus, Cliff, Sully, Steven, Cole, Shaun, and a few members of Bobby's guards—his betas and his omega.

Azil conducted himself calmly, with more dignity than Solomon saw most people comport themselves with.

After almost three hours of grilling, Solomon put his foot down. "We're worn out, and I want to take Azil home. The kids will be up soon, too."

Everyone agreed to continue the discussion later in the day.

Bobby sent out shifters to patrol the grounds and search for trespassers. "We'll find that curandera and any guards sent with her," he vowed.

Remus frowned.

Solomon wondered what that was about but didn't feel it was his place to ask.

He and Azil, along with Steven, Shaun and Cole, reached the house not long before sunrise.

Adal and Dorso greeted them with hugs before Adal shooed them off to bed. "The kids can wait a little longer to see you and to meet Azil."

"Our room is on the ground floor," Solomon said as he guided Azil through the house. "I didn't want to be upstairs in case something happened here. Kid got up early and figured out the door locks, that kind of thing. Now they're all old enough to know better than to sneak out. Except of course that's what teenagers do, so it happens on occasion. I think they try it just to keep me on my toes." Or maybe because they need more freedom. Solomon really had to think about that.

"This is it. We'll get you clothes and anything else you want. The bathroom is attached, so we have it to ourselves." Solomon stopped by the bed, his attention caught by the big, pump-style bottle of lube. "Aw, gods. Please don't tell me Adal did that."

Azil picked the bottle up. "This is big, but not vat size, or fifty-five gallon drum size. It'll do to start, though, right?"

Solomon could get over being traumatized by one of his brothers supplying him with lube when Azil looked at him with that eager, hungry expression. "Might last us a week."

Azil blushed adorably and put the bottle down. "Can we use it now?"

"How about a shower first? I'd love to get you naked, wet and sudsy." Solomon winked.

Azil's cheeks went from pastel pink to neon pink. "Oh. That would be good. We probably don't smell very nice."

Solomon gave the hem of Azil's shirt a tug. "I want to lick your hole until it's open for me."

Azil's eyes rounded. "Ohhh. Then definitely a shower first."

Solomon steered him into the bathroom, where Azil kept darting quick peeks at him. Azil's interest was adorable.

Solomon undressed quickly. Azil had already seen his scars. There was no sense in being shy now. "Something on your mind?" he asked when Azil hesitated to get into the shower.

"I didn't know people did things like lick each other there," Azil finally said. His blush had spread all the way down to his belly.

Solomon didn't miss the way Azil clenched his buttocks when he said that, either. "We can lick each other anywhere, but that's called rimming, and it's definitely on the top of my list of things to do to you. If it helps, I haven't done it, either. Or had it done to me. I'm just as inexperienced as you are."

Azil shoved his pants down. His cock was hard, a column of ivory topped with a pretty pink head. "Can I do it to you?"

Solomon did some clenching himself. "If you want. Doesn't have to be this time. I plan on doing just what I said, licking and working your hole open until it's ready for something much bigger than my tongue."

Azil looked down at Solomon's cock. "That's a lot bigger than a tongue. Thick, too. Made my jaw ache in a good way when I was sucking on it."

Solomon was done with the talking part. He grabbed Azil by one arm and turned the water on.

Then he kissed Azil until they were both trembling. "Shower," Solomon ground out.

They got in, the water too cold but neither of them protesting. Solomon wanted Azil too bad to draw the washing out for very long. Azil must have felt the same way. They scrubbed each other quickly, touching and caressing from time to time, but for the most part, rushing through.

Solomon shut the water off and didn't bother with towels. He got a handful of Azil's balls. "Bed, now."

Azil's breath hitched and he bobbed his head jerkily.

Solomon let go. He watched Azil, appreciating the fluid movements, the flex of muscle under freckled skin. There wasn't a square inch of Azil that didn't have a freckle on it. Solomon vowed to himself to taste every single one of them at some point. Then he crawled onto the bed after Azil and stretched out beside him.

He cupped Azil's chin and stroked his cheek. It should have seemed weird feeling such an intense connection with someone he'd only met a couple of days ago. But the mate bond was running strong between them, annihilating all of Solomon's defenses.

When they kissed, Azil shivered and reached for him. Solomon understood that as he settled a hand on Azil's hip. He needed to hold on, too, because he felt as if he could just float away on the sensations flowing through him.

He'd worried he would feel weird having sex in the house. That was not proving to be the case.

Solomon's inhibitions had fallen away with their clothing. He did pause to make sure he'd locked the door. Assured that their privacy had been secured, he was ready for anything. Solomon rolled over until he was stretched out on top of Azil. He kept the brunt of his weight off the smaller man, bracing himself on his elbows.

But, oh, they connected in all the right spots.

And the whimper from Azil was gratifyingly erotic.

Solomon couldn't hold back a moan of his own when Azil nibbled on his collarbone. Then Azil sucked there, which drove more desperate sounds past Solomon's lips.

Azil brushed his lips over Solomon's skin. "Beautiful."

The rasp of Azil's breath caused him to shiver. Solomon struggled to gather his quickly scattering wits. He needed to get a handle on his body before he came and embarrassed himself. Plus, he'd promised to do something very specific to Azil.

He caught hold of Azil's wrists and pinned them up by his head. Solomon purred again and licked from the divot of Azil's collarbone to right beneath his chin, where he nipped sharply.

Azil was being reduced to a squeaking, needy man, eager and writhing for Solomon.

Solomon kissed him, slick tongue twining with Azil's and delving into every part of Azil's mouth. When he had Azil completely breathless, Solomon raised his head.

"So perfect," Solomon murmured. He dropped whisper-soft kisses over Azil's cheeks, the top of his nose, his closed eyelids. "All mine, all yours," he continued. Solomon was still too close to coming for his own comfort.

Azil's hard length was wet-tipped and smearing pre-cum on Solomon's belly. The smell of it, the feel of it, was pushing Solomon closer and closer to that orgasmic edge.

"I want you. Want you so bad, Azil." The idea of taking him flitted through Solomon's mind, but he needed to do more for Azil. Give more.

"I trust you," Azil said in his ear. "Let me give myself to you."

Rather than answer, Solomon moaned and arched his neck. He rolled them over and let Azil lie on him.

Azil sucked on his Adam's apple then dragged his teeth down, down over Solomon's chest to one taut nipple. Just as he sealed his lips around it, a shriek from upstairs split the air.

"Crap!" Solomon sprang up, sending Azil sprawling and nearly head butting him at the same time. "Sorry! Sorry—"

"Solomon." Azil's voice cut through Solomon's budding panic.

"What? I need—" he began.

"Adal and Dorso have it under control. Listen." Azil canted his head and Solomon did the same.

Nothing but laughter and the low chatter of voices reached him. "I can still hear them."

"Noise," Azil muttered. "Is there something to…to muffle our noise?"

"Noise," Solomon agreed. "Brilliant. You are brilliant, Azil." He got up and found his iPod. "This won't take but a sec."

He put it on the docking station and set the music to play loud enough to drown out the sounds of his siblings. "Come here," he urged, holding a hand out to Azil. "Mark me."

Solomon instantly had himself a horny, happy man in his arms. They fell back onto the bed, and Solomon put Azil on top again. Azil immediately began sucking up marks down his neck.

At the same time he rolled Solomon's nipples between his fingers, Solomon spread his legs wide, planting his heels and humping up against the wonderfully hard cock aligned with his.

After several minutes, Solomon flipped them. He licked Azil's lips, then his neck. The place where he'd bitten Azil was healed already. Solomon dragged his teeth over it.

"Please," Azil begged.

"You'll come," Solomon told him.

"I'll stay hard. I want you, so bad," Azil panted out.

Solomon figured Azil was telling the truth. Gods knew, Solomon could probably stay hard, too, but he wasn't willing to risk it when he wanted inside Azil's sweet butt so badly.

But if Azil was sure...

"I am," Azil said. "Feel the truth, like I feel you in my head."

Solomon struck fast and without warning. His canines dropped before his mouth met Azil's skin.

He bit deep, blood instantly in his mouth, Azil's strangled gasp in his ears, Azil's entire body thrumming for him.

It was a near thing for Solomon. When Azil's spunk spread between them, Solomon almost lost it. He hung on through sheer will.

Biting his mate filled him with a euphoria that was immeasurable. Solomon lapped at the bloody spot and skimmed the rest of the way down from there to Azil's left nipple. Then he worked his way back up again before moving lower, leaving a trail of pink bite marks on Azil's chest.

Azil wasn't complacent in the lovemaking. He touched Solomon, stroking his shoulders, his arms, his back. He wrapped his legs around Solomon's waist, then released him and rubbed all up against Solomon.

Then Azil lightly scratched him with stubby nails.

Solomon couldn't keep his eyes open when they kept trying to roll back in his head. He moaned, hungry for his mate and the pleasure he could bring.

Azil made a pleased sound.

Solomon then moved farther down. He licked a path to Azil's spunk-splattered stomach. There he cleaned up every bit of the salty mess before zeroing in on Azil's belly button.

He delved his tongue in the little divot. Solomon would never have thought such a thing could be erotic, but through their mental link, he could feel that it sent waves of arousal crashing over Azil. Solomon murmured happily then moved down farther still.

Solomon cupped Azil's butt and pulled at his cheeks. He wanted to tell Azil how beautiful he looked there, how perfect that tiny, pink pucker was, but couldn't articulate anything at all.

Instead, he curled Azil's hips up, tipping Azil's butt off the mattress. Without warning, he began lapping at Azil's balls.

Azil jolted, the pleasure bright and hot as it shot from him to Solomon.

Solomon ran his thumbs over Azil's hole while at the same time, he sucked Azil's sac into his mouth.

"Solomon, please, suck me," Azil got out. "Touch me, like you... Like you said."

"You want my mouth here?" he asked, having released Azil's balls. He touched the tempting furled skin of Azil's opening. "My fingers? My dick?"

Azil moaned and that little pucker clenched. "Yes, please!"

"All of it?"

"Solomon—" Azil growled.

Solomon was so pleased by that show of spirit that he flipped Azil right over onto his belly, then pushed his butt cheeks apart.

"Like this?" he asked, but rather than give Azil a chance to answer, Solomon licked Azil's crease from the top to his hole. There he flicked his tongue as Azil gasped.

Solomon tugged on his hips.

Azil came up onto his knees. "Oh gods, oh gods," he chanted.

Solomon took a moment to admire the view. He kept Azil's cheeks pressed far apart, stretching his opening just a bit. "You look so good like this." He wished he knew how to talk dirty, because he really wanted to tell Azil just how hot he was, and all the fun, dirty things Solomon wanted to do to him.

But the words wouldn't come, and Solomon had better things to do with his mouth anyway.

He pressed his face into Azil's crack and rubbed. Azil smelled like the Ivory soap they'd used in the shower, but there was an underlying aroma that was simply Azil himself.

"Solomon!" Azil yelped, rocking back against him.

Solomon couldn't restrain himself any longer. He licked and licked over Azil's pucker until it softened enough for him to slip his tongue in.

Azil gasped and rocked his hips. "Ohmygodsohmygodsohmygods," came from him in a nonstop garble.

Solomon dug his toes against the mattress, trying to keep himself from scrambling up and just pounding into Azil's body. He told himself to slow down, and he curled his tongue, teasing around the inner rim of Azil's opening.

Azil bucked.

Solomon liked that reaction. He rimmed Azil with more enthusiasm, pushing in as deep as he could, twirling his tongue, flicking it, sucking on the softening skin around the outside. He slipped a hand beneath Azil and cupped his nuts, giving them a gentle tug.

Azil mewled and tried to ride his tongue.

Solomon released Azil's balls and instead fisted Azil's cock. It was so hard no one would have ever guessed that Azil had climaxed only minutes beforehand.

His wasn't the only one painfully hard. Solomon felt the ache all the way to his gut, his need for release was so great.

But not as great as his need to please Azil.

He kept rimming Azil, letting him rock back and spear himself on Solomon's tongue. Until Azil asked for more, then demanded it.

"Solomon, now!" Azil almost snapped.

Solomon wasn't going to just pound away at that tiny hole. He did, however, slide two spit-slicked fingers into it. "Get the lube," he said as Azil's silky inner walls clamped down on his digits. "Gods, hurry up."

Azil stretched and reached the lube. He grabbed it then sort of tossed, sort of rolled it back to Solomon.

Solomon had to stop fingering Azil in order to get everything all slick. He did it fast, smearing the viscous stuff on his cock, getting his fingers coated, too.

Then he pushed the two back in. "Like this, honey?"

Azil craned his neck, staring at Solomon. "Honey?"

Solomon smiled and pumped his digits in faster, harder.

Azil's eyes rolled and he plunked his head back onto the pillow.

Solomon felt around and found the small gland he'd read about online. He'd never tried finding his own, hadn't poked around there at all on himself. So he'd been saving himself for his first... Oh well. Solomon was glad he'd held off.

And he was absolutely thrilled with the way Azil keened when his prostate was caressed.

He did it a few more times then he had to give in to his own needs, too. "Azil, I want— Are you ready?"

Azil huffed and rolled his hips forward.

Solomon's digits slipped free.

"Am I ready?" Azil asked. He flopped over onto his back and held his arms open. "Come here."

Solomon really liked the confidence he was seeing in Azil. "Gladly."

He positioned himself between Azil's thighs.

Azil raised his legs up, uncertainty in his expression. "I— How do I—?"

"However you want," Solomon answered. "You can put them on my shoulders, around my waist, up like this." He pushed until Azil's knees were pressed to his own chest. The move tipped Azil's butt up nicely. "This is a really, really perfect way to start."

"Okay." Azil held his legs up.

Solomon ran a finger down from the top of Azil's cock to his hole. "I like this. It displays everything so beautifully."

"I wish you'd do more than look," Azil muttered.

Solomon couldn't hold back a quick laugh, then he was lining his dick up to that glistening little pucker. He was torn, wanting to watch it slide in, wanting to stare into Azil's eyes. Solomon thrust gently, saw the head stretching Azil's ring.

He looked up just in time to see Azil's eyes roll back in his head.

"Gawds," Azil drawled, neck arching, butt wiggling. "More, please."

Solomon could do that. More worked nicely for him, too. He settled his hands above Azil's shoulders and sank into the welcoming heat of his body. "Fu—" Solomon closed his eyes as he bit back the rest of the bad word. He didn't say it, but he also didn't have anything suitable for the mind-boggling experience of Azil's velvety muscles constricting around his dick, pulling him in, setting every nerve ending to brilliant, flaring bands of pleasure.

Solomon's eyes shot open when Azil moaned and wrapped his legs around Solomon.

"Come here, please," Azil whispered, his face flushed pink, mouth wet, too tempting to resist.

Solomon lowered himself down and took a kiss, then another. Slowly, he began to move, pulling out an inch or two, then gliding back until his balls were pressed to Azil's butt.

He fisted a hand in Azil's hair. Their kiss turned fierce, both biting, nipping, needing.

Solomon began thrusting with more force, less caution, the need between them flowing from one to another via their mate bond.

When Solomon began to grunt with every deep drive in, he pulled Azil's head aside. "Mark me like I did you," he demanded, arching his neck.

Azil yowled just before he bit.

Hot pain mingled with bliss. Solomon lost what grip he had on his control. His cat took over, though he didn't shift forms. His animalistic nature rose to the surface regardless. Solomon snarled as he lost himself in his mate and the ecstasy spiraling back and forth between them.

He couldn't seem to stop thrusting. Solomon needed in deeper, needed more of Azil. Then he was suddenly there, in that perfect moment where one rises out of their body on a cloud of pleasure. Beating off had never been like that, nothing had. This was the first climax Solomon had experienced that was truly earth-shaking for him.

Azil cried out. The scent of his cum was pungent and perfect, and spurred another jet of spunk from Solomon's cock. Together they clung and writhed until Solomon's strength left him and he feared he was going to collapse on top of Azil.

Slowly, he eased his dick from Azil's hole. Solomon didn't feel his body was wholly functioning yet, and his movements were rather jerky. He watched Azil's face for signs of pain, but Azil only shivered and moaned.

Solomon settled himself beside his mate. "Come here?" he asked.

Azil curled into him without a second's hesitation.

"Rest," Solomon said, and he wasn't certain if it was a question or a suggestion.

It ceased to matter as sleep tugged him under.

# Chapter Ten

Hours later, Azil sat up in the bed. Solomon was there, sleeping, looking so relaxed Azil hated to wake him.

But... Azil eyed the shadow under the door.

"Solomon," Azil whispered, nudging Solomon in the ribs.

Solomon hummed and smacked his lips before opening one eye just a tiny bit. "Hn?"

Azil pointed at the door. "Someone is waiting out there. I can see their shadow under the door."

Solomon yawned and stretched. He kicked off the sheet, baring his gorgeous, nude body. The scars didn't detract from Solomon's form. Instead, Azil thought they showed off his strength. The things the man had survived would have killed almost anyone else.

"I like the way you think of me," Solomon said.

"Solomon! You're up!" someone yelled from the other side of the door. "Let me in!"

Azil had never moved so fast in his life as he did when he heard a young child's voice calling out. He was halfway dressed in under ten seconds.

"It's locked," Solomon pointed out, but he got up as well. "Give me a second, Rhea. I've got my mate in here."

"Your what?" Rhea demanded. "No! You have us!"

"Oh. Er." Azil stopped in the midst of putting his shirt on. "I should stay in here and let you —"

"No way," Solomon grumbled. "She's been full of herself lately." Solomon leaped on the bed then off again, landing on Azil's side. He cupped Azil's cheek. "She's a child who's always been cared for and coddled. She isn't a bad kid, but she can be challenging. She'll love you in no time at all." Solomon pressed his forehead to Azil's. "Don't let her bully or intimidate you."

"I won't." *I hope. Oh gods, what am I doing?* Azil kept the thoughts to himself. He was more afraid of facing the little girl on the other side of the door than he had been when he'd faced the queen.

"Rhea, you'd better behave," Solomon warned. He kissed Azil's cheek and winked at him.

Every time Solomon did that — winked — Azil's heart fluttered. The first time it had happened, Azil had feared he'd discovered a birth defect or something. Now he knew it was just Solomon's effect on him.

"You don't need a mate," the girl said petulantly.

"Stop being such a brat," someone else said — a boy, Azil thought.

"Don't call me names, butthead!" Rhea exclaimed.

Azil glanced at the bed. "I bet the blankets and sheets are still warm."

"Azil, don't even think about it." Solomon didn't sound angry.

A check of his expression showed amusement.

Azil rolled his eyes. "I'm tired."

"You're trying to hide, and if you do that, she'll have won the first round," Solomon warned. "Come on. Finish getting dressed before Rhea and Dmitri get into a physical fight."

Azil tugged his shirt down just as a loud thump sounded against the door.

"Solomon!" Dmitri wailed. "She bit me!"

"I—" Rhea didn't finish whatever she'd intended to say.

Solomon sighed. "Bet Steven's out there now."

As far as Azil was concerned, that was a good thing. "He lives here too, him and his mates?"

"Yeah, of course." Solomon strode to the door.

Azil joined him. "Then he gets to help with the kids."

Solomon chuckled. "Oh yeah." He unfastened the lock. "Ready for this?"

"Probably not, but you won't let me hide, so…" Azil felt rather daring, teasing like that.

Solomon beamed at him. "I do like your attitude, Az."

Azil liked it, too.

Solomon opened the door. No one was right outside of it any longer.

There were voices coming from close by.

"They're in the living room," Solomon said. "And the kitchen. And the dining room."

Azil felt himself pale. There *were* a lot of people in the house. It shouldn't have been a shock, and yet it was. He'd not had time to adjust to anything—but he'd rather be where he was than back with the clan. So Azil held his head high, kept his shoulders back, his spine straight. He could do this. He *would* do this.

Besides, they were kids. That wasn't a reassuring thought. He knew how cruel kids could be.

"You're going to worry yourself to bits," Solomon murmured, taking his hand. "Relax."

"It's important," Azil offered. "This is your family."

"And you're my mate. We'll be fine." Solomon linked their fingers.

They entered the kitchen first. Cole, Shaun and a young lady were bickering over recipes. The squabbling stopped when Azil and Solomon were spotted.

The girl tossed her glossy black hair back and smiled brightly. "So this is your mate, hmm, Solomon? Azil, right?" she said as she approached.

Azil had to clear his throat after his first attempt at speech ended in a squeak. "Yes. Azil."

"I'm Kylie."

Azil had been expecting a handshake, maybe. He was not prepared for the hug as Kylie launched herself at him.

"Welcome to the family! Solomon deserves someone special. I'm sure you do, too." She didn't release him.

Azil realized she was taller than him, and muscular as well. Not bulky, but there was no softness to her form.

"So, tell me what you would rather have? Lemon bars, oatmeal raisin cookies, or apple pie?" Kylie asked. "We were all trying to figure out which would say welcome to the family best."

"Uh." Azil didn't know what any of those things were, so he just picked one. "The lemon bars?"

"Yes!" Kylie did let go of him then. She bounced and pumped a fist in the air. "I was right!"

"Well, she does make awesome lemon bars," Shaun said. "And that means we don't have to cook." He and Cole high-fived each other. "Yes!"

"Someone has to do dinner." Kylie smirked and walked to the refrigerator.

"Crap." Shaun sighed. "Okay, Azil. Tacos or spaghetti?"

Cole and Shaun stared at him expectantly.

Azil gave Solomon a mental poke. *"Help?"*

*"Tacos. Definitely tacos. Fajita tacos."*

"Fajita tacos," Azil answered.

Cole narrowed his eyes. "That's cheating, Solomon. You know I make the tacos."

"And they're really, really good." Solomon rubbed his stomach. "Wish we had some right now."

"Eat cereal," Cole groused. "Tacos will be ready in a couple of hours."

Solomon let go of Azil's hand. "Why don't you take a seat on one of the bar stools, honey." Then, to Cole, "We'll have sandwiches, thanks. Steven handling Rhea and Dmitri?"

"Yeah, he is." Shaun helped Solomon gather the makings for sandwiches. "Rhea doesn't argue with him as much as she does with you."

Solomon set the bread and condiments on the kitchen island. "I don't understand why she's become so angry. Is she worse than the others were at her age, or am I just paranoid?"

"We've all spoiled her," Cole said. "She was so cute and cuddly and we all felt bad for her. Not that you hadn't done a fantastic job of raising her—she just evoked that kind of sympathy in everyone."

"We're not doing her any favors by letting it continue." Solomon handed Azil a plate. "There's ham, salami, turkey, cheese. Do you want any lettuce? Or pickles? Tomato?"

Azil wasn't used to having so many choices. He just ate what he was given. Even at the diner, he'd had Solomon order for him.

Solomon's expression softened and he touched Azil's hand. "There's no wrong answer. Just, try what you want to. If you don't like it, don't eat it. Food should be enjoyed."

Azil did enjoy it, very much. He even managed to wave at kids that came to see who he was. Most of them were very friendly, hugging him like Kylie had. Rhea was a holdout, glaring at him instead. So was Erdwin, though he seemed more inclined to shyness than to the jealousy Rhea exhibited.

Steven eventually shooed all the kids out of the kitchen, except for Kylie and Erdwin, who was helping her bake.

"So what was Rhea's punishment?"

Steven glanced at Solomon. "The 3DS got taken away, and her TV rights. She bit Dmitri, and at age eight, she knows better."

"I don't understand her level of acting out," Solomon said.

Azil wondered if anyone had asked Rhea directly what her problem was or, less confrontationally, why she was unhappy.

Solomon smacked his palm against his forehead. "Jeez. No, I don't think so."

Azil realized he'd not shielded the thought. "I wasn't trying to intrude."

Steven arched an eyebrow.

Solomon rubbed his forehead. "Ouch. I have to stop doing that. And, Azil, you're part of this family. Being a new member, you might just have insights we lack."

That warmed Azil all the way down to his toes. It made him happy.

"He has a suggestion?" Steven asked.

Azil willed himself not to blush. "I just wondered if anyone had talked to her and asked her why she's unhappy."

"How can she be unhappy? She has everything!" Steven's exasperation lent itself to his voice, making it dagger-sharp. "She has no reason to *not* be happy."

"That you know of," Azil said quietly. "I would think that, perhaps a little girl, while able to love the brothers raising her, might have questions about her mother, for one thing."

Solomon grimaced. "That was on my mind before I was kidnapped. I don't want to break this family up, not at all, but..." He exhaled. "But if there are any of the kids' mothers out there, alive and wanting to know their child, we should... We should try to find them. Offer to let them live here, if they'd do that. I don't want to lose anyone."

Azil did carefully guard his thoughts then, because kids grew up. They found other people—in his clan, the boys were given to other people, but he knew that wasn't the way of it elsewhere. The point was, children became adults, and they had their own lives. Surely Solomon knew that.

Solomon didn't look like he knew that, or wanted it to happen. "Do all of your siblings live here? Even the adult ones?" Azil asked.

Solomon blinked, appearing startled. "Yes. Didn't I say so? Maybe not. We haven't had a lot of time to get to know each other."

And Azil wasn't going to start poking his nose in the family side of things yet. Solomon was right—they didn't know each other well.

Though Azil could tell Solomon just what his cum tasted like, and the sounds he made when he climaxed. The way he tensed, his muscles rippling and —

*"Azil, gods, stop! I've got a hard-on in the kitchen!"* Solomon might have protested, but he slid a hand very high up Azil's thigh.

"Has anyone found anything out about the curandera and the guards from the Vento clan?" Solomon asked, inching his hand up even farther. The side of it brushed against Azil's balls. "And what about Rolly?"

Steven leaned over the bar and smirked. "Getting a handful, little brother?"

Solomon grinned, but moved his hand down a tad. "Ah, but he's more than a handful."

"Solomon!" Azil smacked his arm.

Solomon gave him an innocent look. "What? I'm bragging. I should brag. I know what you've got —"

Azil thumped him again.

"I don't think your mate's amused," Steven noted.

Azil wasn't amused, not at all.

"Oh, shoot. I'm sorry, Az." Solomon stopped caressing his leg and instead cupped his jaw. "I didn't — I was just teasing. I'm so happy to have you here, and I should have remembered that this would be difficult for you. Not just the kids part. The whole deal."

"Remus said he sensed a new power in the area," Steven said, either tired of listening to Azil and Solomon's chatter or trying to move past it. "And yeah, he said it's evil. I asked him outright if it was stronger than him and he said no, but that something was off. He still can't see the outcome of this, or anything about it. It's really bothering him."

"Yeah, he's been chanting and pulling us in for ceremonies every night," Cole added. He glanced toward Kylie and Erdwin. "Um."

Azil was confused for a moment but Solomon wasn't.

He kept his voice very low when he spoke. "I'll talk to Elena, Kylie and the twins about her tonight, after the younger ones are in bed."

*Irial. Solomon's mom. Of course.*

"Erdwin, do you want to find out who your mother is, if we can do that?" Solomon asked.

Erdwin dropped the bowl he'd been holding. It clattered against the countertop but didn't break. He looked from Solomon to Azil, then back to Solomon. After a half minute of nibbling on his lip, Erdwin answered. "I—yes? But I don't think Bashuan let her live. I would still like to know about her."

"We'll see what we can do. I should have asked sooner." Solomon looked at Kylie.

She crossed her arms over her chest. "You didn't ask me. What do you know about our mom?"

"What I told you before—that she's dead," Solomon replied bluntly. "That isn't new information. However, her name was Irial, and her sister sold her to Bashuan."

Kylie's features sharpened with anger, the scent of that emotion bitter in the kitchen. "Sold her to that bastard? What kind of hateful—?" She took a deep breath, exhaled, then took another.

Azil hated that he had any part in this, but he did. "The queen of the clan I was raised in. She sent me, along with four of her trusted guards, to bring her Solomon. She intends to have all of her sister's children. I don't know her intent, but I wouldn't believe it to be for any sort of good."

"Don't start in on Azil," Solomon said before anyone else could speak. "You don't know what it was like for him, and he didn't know about Irial until I did. Leeloo told us."

"Leeloo?" Kylie asked. "Wait. You know what? Just wait and let me get these lemon bars on, then I want to hear everything."

# Chapter Eleven

Steven left the kitchen after telling Solomon he'd be back later. Cole and Shaun accompanied him.

"We're going hunting, aren't we?" Cole asked, sounding quite happy about it.

"We are," Steven confirmed. "Remus said he can feel an evil presence nearby. They may not be on the pack lands — in fact, I'm sure they aren't. Remus has wards in place, spells, charms, whatever. He'd know if the property was breached. But, if someone is watching, they can't be too far off, and we're going to find them, and end them, and be done with this shit."

"Sounds like a good plan to me."

"Me too," Shaun said. "It makes me nervous, Remus not being able to see anything, and not being able to reach Rolly? How does that happen?"

"It shouldn't happen, but if Rolly is in deep mediation, he could be unreachable, I guess," Cole explained. "A true meditative state can be maintained for a long time, actually. Rolly, I didn't expect him to be gone this long. I thought he'd be back. Thought he'd be home years ago." He shook his head.

Shaun made a weary sound.

Steven knew Cole missed Rolly. They were close brothers, but for whatever reason, Rolly had left shortly after Solomon and the kids had settled in. Something about that, the timing of it, seemed odd, but there was nothing specific Steven could pinpoint for that feeling.

He decided to concentrate on the task he'd set before himself. "We're going to check the entire perimeter, from half a mile out. See if we pick up anything that way. Bobby's wanting to go after that clan for kidnapping Solomon. The only thing keeping him here right now is the threat of more kidnappings, and the evil Remus senses."

"And we're all a little freaked out over Dad not being able to pick up anything else about what's going on. Even Cliff is getting concerned, and he's usually not worried about anything but when he'll get his next meal." Cole chuckled. "I feel better knowing it's not 'cause Dad's going to die or anything. He said that wasn't why he wasn't able to get any information. It has to do with the Fates not wanting him to know shit."

"The way things work out," Shaun muttered. "Your dad has to be okay. None of us would know what to do without him giving us advice."

"He's going to live forever," Cole said. He tipped his head up, staring at the sky. "That's not tempting the Fates or anything. That's just letting everyone know that y'all are kind, loving ladies. And I'd really appreciate it if you'd let my dad live for a very, very long time, if not forever. Cliff, too."

"That's as close to a prayer as I've ever heard from you, man." Shaun patted Cole's back. "You must really be worried."

"Aren't you?" Cole asked.

Shaun nodded. "Not like you, I guess. I just always believe it's going to work out for the best, and the good people will win. I *know* that doesn't always happen. That's why I quit watching the news. Too depressing. Still choose to believe it'll be the good side winning when it comes to us and ours, though."

"That's a good way to believe," Steven said to Shaun. "I like it. I'm not sure I'm the good guy yet, but I'll get there."

Cole bumped shoulders with him. "You're definitely a good guy."

"And sexy," Shaun added. "Don't forget sexy."

Steven snorted. If they had the time, he'd have whisked his mates off and spent the next twenty-four hours or so loving on them. There were important things that needed doing first, starting with finding the curandera and any shifters alien to Bobby's pack.

"Does Bobby know what we're doing?"

Steven glanced at Shaun, who'd asked the question. "He knows. I didn't want his betas and the other morons that help them to get in our way." Steven touched his side. "I'm not going to push Bobby. He's earned my respect."

"And it only took him years," Shaun said, chuckling afterwards.

Steven's lips twitched as he fought a grin. "Well, I like to take my time to decide how I feel about people who aren't family, or mates."

"You took long enough to decide about us. You don't trust anyone quickly." Cole didn't sound upset over it.

Considering the way they'd met, with Steven trying to take out both Shaun and Cole, not understanding that they were his mates, well... It'd been a rough beginning.

"Bobby can be full of himself. It clashes with my cockiness," Steven admitted, knowing he wasn't sharing anything new with those words. "Men and their egos, as Kylie always says."

Cole flapped a hand in the air, making a rolling motion. "Like she and Elena don't get all puffed up, pissy, and competitive over everything. They're like two cats with their tails tangled together. Always swiping at each other."

"They're too much alike," Shaun observed. "Same with Bobby and you," he said to Steven.

Steven supposed there were worse comparisons. He still had to bristle on principle. Cole and Shaun both laughed at him.

"Turds."

"Sure, and you love us." Shaun kissed his cheek. "So are we ready to shift and run? Make our family and pack safe again?"

Shaun was right. No one was safe when an unknown threat was out there. Yes, they had a name and an idea of what and who wanted to cause harm, but no true knowledge of the person, or the guards if they were lurking, waiting. Steven wasn't going to have his family harmed again, and when Solomon had been taken, he'd nearly lost his mind with worry. Yes, it was definitely time to end whoever, whatever, sought to hurt the people Steven loved.

He stopped by the last outbuilding on the south end of the property. The fall weather meant days not in the triple digits, but not exactly cool weather. It just wasn't hellish. He was sweaty, and eager to sink his claws into the enemy. Gods knew he'd killed other people for much lesser slights.

He bent and began unlacing his boots. "It'll be dark in a few hours. Let's shift and get to work."

"And he expects me to think when he's bent over like that," Cole joked. "But fine. I can control my libido. For a little while."

Steven's groin tingled with arousal but he tamped it down. Now wasn't the time, and Cole was only trying to interject some lightheartedness into what was going to become a very serious, deadly afternoon.

\* \* \* \*

"Kylie, I'd prefer to do this when Elena and the twins are here," Solomon began, but he held up a hand when she would have protested. "You know the basics, and that's really all we have. A name—Irial—and that she was sold to Bashuan by her sister, Wyanem. Wyanem leads a clan rife with misandry. Azil and the other men there are no more than slaves. For whatever reason, Wyanem wants us, Irial's children. I think she fears retaliation." He stopped and rubbed at his forehead. His mind was racing. So was his heart. Steven and his mates had left with a purposeful stride, and it worried him.

"Look, Azil and I will discuss this later. I need to go see what Steven's up to." Solomon stood.

Azil did as well.

Kylie drummed her fingers on the table. "Okay, I'm just excited to find out anything about our past. I know it scares you, especially when it comes to the younger kids, but it's the right thing to do, trying to find the mothers, if any are alive. I'd think it unlikely with Bashuan having been the twisted bastard he was—and I'm not doing laundry for that. I stated a truth, nothing more." Then she made a shooing motion at them. "Go on. Take another sandwich or two. Neither of you ate enough, and I agree, Steven's got some kick-butt plan in motion. He's trying to take it all on himself, and his mates, to save everyone."

"He doesn't have to do that alone." Solomon tried not to be irritated. He wanted Steven to see him as an equal but understood there was a difference in their strength and ability to give themselves over to violence.

But that didn't mean Solomon couldn't do it. He'd killed before. He'd do it again for his family and mate's sake.

"Elena and I will watch the kiddos. Adal and Dorso should be up soon, too. We'll be fine here." Kylie got up and walked to the stove. She put a hand on Erdwin's shoulder. "Erdwin and I will finish making the world's best lemon bars."

"Keep everyone inside, and the doors locked. Windows, too." Solomon ignored the glare that got him. He knew Kylie was capable. He'd worry regardless. He picked up a sandwich and handed it to Azil before getting himself one. "Can you grab us a bottle of water each from the fridge?"

"Sure." Azil crossed over to the refrigerator and took out the first bottle, which he tossed to Solomon. He grabbed a second bottle. "All ready."

"Would you let Bobby know where we are, Kylie? Just that we're going to help Steven and his mates?" It would be wise to check in with their alpha.

"I could go with y'all," Erdwin said, glancing at them.

Solomon didn't want his gentle younger brother exposed to what might happen out there. "I'd appreciate it if you would stay here and help keep everyone safe."

Erdwin ducked his head, his black curls sliding over his back and shoulders. "I'm not weak."

Solomon wanted to groan. Now wasn't the time for this. Reminding himself to be patient — Erdwin had a kind heart and good intentions — he strode over and set his sandwich and drink on the counter. "Come here." He opened his arms.

Erdwin all but flew into them, holding him in return. Erdwin was very thin, his arms barely showing any musculature at all, but he was very strong for all that he didn't look it. "I'm not useless."

"No, you aren't." Solomon stroked some of those soft curls. "You really aren't. Would you send Dmitri or Xander out there, or Geneva? Any of the younger kids?"

Erdwin sniffled. "I see where you're going with this."

Solomon was sure Erdwin did. He was still going to clarify it. "I want to protect you, just as you'd protect them. I need you here. If the guards from Wyanem's clan somehow get through to the house, you'll have to fight. Then you fight with everything you have. Have Bobby send a couple of wolf shifters over, too. If anything happens, they can howl louder than any of us felines can yowl. They'll sound an alarm everyone can hear."

"Okay. I—" Erdwin released him partially, resting his hands on Solomon's forearms. He looked at Solomon with big brown eyes that could melt the hardest man's heart. "I just want to be helpful. I'm not a wimp. I'm just shy," he whispered the last word as he peeked past Solomon to Azil.

"Nothing wrong with that." Solomon took the opportunity to try to make an important point. He turned Erdwin's face gently back toward him. "There is nothing wrong with *anything* about you, Erdwin. *Everything* about you is as it should be. Maybe you can stop fighting that and accept it. I do. Everyone who loves you will."

Erdwin's blush raged over his face as his mouth worked, open, shut, open, shut. Finally, he spluttered then coughed. "H-how—?"

"Had to put up your laundry, sweetie. Someone had mixed up our clothes. You were outside with the kids in the pool. I wasn't snooping." Solomon didn't say anything else. He'd found the silky, lacy panties and the makeup hidden beneath them. Solomon kissed Erdwin's brow. "Be who you are."

Erdwin's eyes glistened and tears spilled out. "Oh. Oh. I..." He trembled then latched onto Solomon tightly. "I don't know if I can."

"You can," Solomon assured him. "We love you." He sent a look to Kylie, then Azil.

Both joined them in a group hug, although Azil was a bit timid about it. Still, he took part, and that made Solomon's heart soar with joy. Erdwin cried softly for a few minutes then he sniffled loudly and wiggled, signaling that he was over the hugging part.

"Go. Go on and...and thank you. All of you," Erdwin said. "I'll think about what you said, Solomon."

Solomon nodded. He took his sandwich and water, waited for Azil to grab his food and drink as well, then they left the house, intent on finding out what Steven was up to.

"They're heading out of the dwelling areas to the uninhabited parts of the pack lands. I'd say they're going hunting." Solomon found the neatly piled clothing a few minutes later. "Definitely." He turned to Azil. "Are you ready for this?"

Azil started unbuttoning his shirt. "Maybe I can even be of some assistance since I know the guard drills and patterns, the way they work. I wasn't with them for long, but trained for over a year prior to that in order to learn all the moves and skills a guard must know. And I've met the curandera, Tritaya. I would know her scent."

"Then let's find her." Solomon set down the empty water bottles, taking Azil's from him first. Then he began to remove his shoes and clothing.

When they were both nude, Solomon cupped Azil's nape and drew him in for a fierce kiss. He delved in deep, tasting his mate, needing him, vowing to love on him thoroughly once this situation was resolved.

Azil purred and rubbed against him. He lapped at the spot he'd bitten earlier. "It's already healed!"

Solomon knew it was. "And you seem to have taken on some of my quick healing abilities. I didn't know it was possible, but then again, we're learning that us half-breed shifters are different in more than just appearances."

"My bite did heal very quickly," Azil acknowledged. "I've never been exceptional in any way, so that was new. It does have to be because of you. That's... That's amazing!"

Solomon was glad he could do something like that for his mate. "We need to tell Rolly about it once we finish this. As our shaman, he should be made aware of the way our mate bond has developed. Who knows? Maybe it's an evolution for all shifter kind, not just half-breeds."

"Or maybe you and your siblings *are* the evolution of shifters," Azil said. "What we will eventually become."

Solomon took another kiss. "Maybe we are." And it wasn't a bad thing as far as he was concerned. "I think we'll head in the opposite direction than what Steven and his mates took. Meet them in the middle. Ready?"

"Yes." Azil began to shift.

Solomon was done in less than a heartbeat. He noted that Azil morphed faster this time than he had before. Was that something else that came from them being mates?

*"It must be. I've been consistent with the time it took me to shift since right after I learned how to do it."* Azil gave a rolling stretch, arching deeply and digging his claws into the ground. He truly was a beautiful beast. He flicked his tail.

Solomon looked forward to the day when he could frolic and play with Azil in their shifted forms. Hopefully, it wouldn't be too long before that was possible. Maybe even tomorrow, if they were successful on their hunt today.

"Solomon, Azil, wait."

Solomon spun around. He hadn't heard Remus—or Cliff, who was with him—approach.

Remus looked worried, a frown marring his features, drawing lines across his brow. Cliff didn't seem any different than usual.

"We're coming with you." That was all Remus said before he shifted, his clothing falling off him. Cliff's did as well.

Solomon assumed some sort of magic was involved with that.

Remus and Cliff made a glorious pair. Cliff shifted into his wolf. As the only known dual shifter, he could choose a feline form to take.

Solomon and Azil took the lead for a little while, until Cliff barreled past them.

Remus loped after Cliff.

When night fell, they hadn't yet met up with Steven, Cole and Shaun. The moon was a bare sliver in the night sky, and a cool breeze reminded Solomon that not every day in South Texas was miserably hot.

A lone howl quickly followed by another rent the air. Solomon, along with his hunting group, froze, the fur along his spine standing up. *"Cole. That's Cole and Shaun."* And they were howls of alarm, not greeting or anything else.

Solomon started to run just as another set of howls sounded. His heart stopped when he realized they were coming from the direction of the house.

# Chapter Twelve

Steven howled again, hoping the pack would hear. He and his mates had walked right into an ambush. There was no scent or tracks to warn them. The curandera who worked with the jaguar clan was more talented than he'd hoped.

And now he, Shaun and Cole had over a dozen jaguars surrounding them. Steven thought they could take the cats, but what was holding him back was the one jaguar shifter who was still in human form. She held a big-ass gun and had it aimed at him and his mates. Steven was fast, he was deadly. He still didn't have the speed of a bullet.

"Howl all you want, wolf. I'm not the only one out here with one of these," the woman said, hoisting the weapon up an inch. "We know of your shaman. Even he isn't bulletproof."

Steven wouldn't bet on that.

"Perhaps we will bring you three back to our clan," she mused. Then she pulled a second weapon off her hip. "Along with the whole houseful of kids. We need fresh blood."

Steven vibrated with rage. He wanted to tear the jaguar to pieces.

"Cats living with wolves." She sneered. "What do you think comes from such warped cohabitation? Death, that's what you should get." She raised the second weapon. "Consider this me being lenient."

Steven dodged the first dart. He knocked Shaun aside, and Cole dove to the left. The second and third dart hit Steven mid-chest. He yowled and leaped at the nearest jaguar. If he was going to be killed, if his mates were to be taken from him, he was going to bring down hell and destruction on the enemy.

*"Kill them all!"* he thought to his mates. He could feel the poison from the darts spreading, sapping his strength. *Gods, help me. Help me!* He couldn't have survived everything he had just to be taken from the Earth now. His mates would die if he did, and that was unthinkable.

Or they could be killed by the jaguars.

The idea of it incensed Steven, and he ripped through the tough hide of his first victim. Blood spurted out over his muzzle, into his mouth. He tossed his head hard, snapping bones. Claws raked down his side, down his back.

Steven gave himself over to the red haze of fury that pounded into his skull. He would kill, and nothing would stop him.

\* \* \* \*

*"Go back to the house!"*

Even though Remus was in animal form, Solomon heard the words clearly in his head. As far as he'd known, only mates could speak to each other in such a way. Remus was obviously powerful enough to make an exception there.

Solomon was torn. He wanted to help Steven, but Remus was right. If the house was under attack, Solomon needed to go protect his family there. Steven had his mates, as well as Cliff and Remus, coming to his aid.

Solomon would put his money on Remus and Cliff any day.

"We'll make sure Bobby knows what's happening," Solomon thought to Azil. One of the downsides to being a feline shifter was the inability to howl. He could, however, make as much noise as possible. The guttural growls came with every exhalation. Solomon strained his vocal cords trying to be louder.

He heard Azil beside him, adding to the noise. Solomon cut across the pack lands. They'd been running along the outskirts of them, so cutting through was a lot faster. It still took them entirely too long in his opinion to get home.

And when they did near the dwellings, he saw other shifters running toward his house. There were so many of them, in fact, that he couldn't see what was happening. It looked like the entire pack was there, ready and willing to defend Solomon's family.

Solomon would have been deeply touched had the scent of smoke not come his way with the shift of the wind. Then he heard it, the word "Fire" being shouted and muttered. Bright orange flames shot up into the sky as a loud explosion tore through the night.

"No!" Solomon shifted, screaming, running, fear propelling him past anyone in his way. He shoved and leaped, dimly aware that Azil was beside him, trying to help clear the way.

People grabbed at him, tried to calm him or whatever. Solomon didn't know or care what they were doing. He just had to reach the house, had to reach his family.

The entire atmosphere seemed to shimmer and warp. Something very wrong was happening. Terror caused a chill to almost paralyze Solomon.

He saw the house. The entire front of it was burning. More flames licked up from the roof toward the sky. People had formed a long line and were throwing buckets of water on it, someone else was spraying a hose. He didn't see his siblings.

"Around back," Azil urged. "Check there! The pool—"

Solomon ran faster than he ever had. He cleared the side of the house. He was drenched in sweat from the heat rolling off the fire. Some of his body hair was likely singed, too. He didn't care.

The backyard was filled with people too. He spotted Bobby shouting out orders. Bobby's hair was burnt, he had dark patches on his body and one on his cheek that didn't look like soot. Bobby saw him immediately and hollered at him.

"Where's Steven? And Remus? Where are their mates?" Bobby demanded. "We need our healer!"

Solomon's stomach rolled. "They're fighting someone. I don't know— We heard the howls here and Remus said come—"

"God damn it!" Bobby roared. "What the fuck is happening!" His anger was flung out on a wave of power. Bobby had never lost control that Solomon knew about. He was certainly on the verge of it now. "Get us help!"

Solomon wasn't sure just who Bobby was yelling at.

Azil grabbed Solomon's arm and pointed. "There."

Solomon ran to his family. He saw Adal, Dorso, Kylie, Elena, Erdwin, the twins—a glance and he knew who was missing. Dmitri and Rhea.

"I tried to get everyone. I tried," Adal said, tears streaking his cheeks. Dorso had him in a tight embrace. "Bobby said he won't stop until he has everyone out."

Solomon turned and saw Bobby run back into the burning house. "Sully?"

Adal sobbed and tipped his head to a still form on the ground. "He's alive, but he's hurt badly. A beam fell."

Solomon's eyes burned from smoke, from tears. "Where—? Do you have any idea where Dmitri and Rhea are?"

"They'd been in their rooms," Erdwin said in a broken voice. His curls were gone, his hair a short, burnt mess. "I went in, I did, but they weren't there. We were just sleeping, and suddenly—" His breath hitched. Great sobs tore out of him.

Solomon wasn't much comfort. His own heart was being ripped from his chest.

Kylie and Elena pulled Erdwin into their arms.

"Please. I tried, Solomon," Erdwin cried.

Solomon forced himself to function past the agony of loss. He wouldn't mourn yet. He needed to believe his brother and sister would be okay. "It isn't your fault, Erdwin. Somehow, these jaguars got past all of us. They are more powerful and dangerous than we thought."

He turned to Azil. "I have to go in."

"I'm coming with you." Azil clenched his jaw. His mind was made up.

Solomon could feel that there'd be no swaying him. That was understandable. Solomon wouldn't have stayed behind had their positions been reversed.

"But someone needs to get Remus," Kylie said. "Sully's hurt bad, and we m-might need h-him for—"

Solomon looked at Erdwin. "You go with Kylie and Elena. Be careful. Be very careful. Get Remus and Cliff. Tell Steven what's happening." Solomon couldn't imagine that Steven hadn't been successful in whatever battle he'd faced. Especially not if Remus and Cliff were helping. That didn't mean that caution wasn't wise. "Watch for anyone. Don't just assume people are on our side. And see if you can take some of the guards with you. A few, at least. Tell them it's Bobby's orders, because that's the truth. He needs Remus here."

And how did Remus not know that?

Solomon couldn't fret over it. He had to find his siblings. "Be safe," he said, then he turned and headed for the burning house.

The heat was indescribable. Solomon wished he'd grabbed a shirt or something to cover his mouth and nose. Azil, too. He turned and Azil shook his head.

*"I'm going with you, now."*

Solomon had to try. *"You could grab something to cover our faces partially."*

*"Will you wait for me?"* Azil asked.

Solomon didn't answer. He wouldn't lie. The need to get to Dmitri and Rhea was too great to hesitate.

He spun back around and ducked into the house. Smoke immediately assaulted him. He'd thought the heat outside was bad, but inside it was like the deepest level of hell.

Azil kept a hand on his back. *"We should crawl. Less smoke."*

Solomon lowered himself down onto his hands and knees. He didn't know whether being nude was a good thing or not. There was nothing to protect his skin. He suspected that if he'd been wearing clothes, they'd have burnt off him shortly.

"Bobby!" he shouted. "Dmitri, Rhea!" Solomon sent the thought out as well, knowing he had no psychic power at all but hoping against hope that the Fates would take mercy upon him.

He could hardly see in front of him, even lower down as he was. *"Stay right with me, Azil. Or please, please, go back outside."*

*"I can't. I have to do this. They're my family, too, aren't they?"*

Solomon didn't push Azil any further on the matter. Azil had a core of integrity that Solomon was coming to discover. He hoped they lived long enough for him to explore it fully.

He heard a scream off to the left. *"Our room! Oh gods, that would be where Rhea went!"* And where Rhea went, Dmitri was never far away. No one would have thought to check Solomon's room first, since he'd been out.

Solomon veered toward his room, going more by memory than anything else. The thick black smoke rolled down and loud, cracking sounds came from overhead. Flames licked at his skin. Pain flared as bright as the fire, but he ignored it. He'd heal, quickly.

*"As will I,"* Azil thought.

Solomon almost stopped moving. *"Are you hurt?"*

*"Mild burns. I can handle this. Go. Let's bring the children to safety."*

"Bobby!" Solomon shouted again.

"In here!" Bobby replied with a raspy yell. "Your room."

Solomon had been right. He scrambled to the bedroom. He'd never been so grateful for taking the bottom floor room for himself. Had they been on the second floor, this would have been much worse. The stairs were likely collapsed or on the verge of it.

In the bedroom, Bobby was on the floor by the closet. "In there. They won't come out. I can't— I—" He nodded to his right arm.

Solomon saw then that he was pinned down, a thick piece of wood having speared through his biceps and into the floor. "Gods," he gasped, nausea turning his gut.

"I'll get him," Azil said.

Solomon turned to the closet. "Rhea, Dmitri, come out. We have to get out of here."

No one answered. With the thick smoke and the heat, Solomon feared the worst. He couldn't hold back tears as he crawled into the small space. His relief at finding Rhea and Dmitri alive was tempered by the sheer terror on their expressions and their inability or refusal to acknowledge him.

"It's me, Solomon. We have to get out of here." He reached for them.

Rhea shrieked, the sound so full of fear it broke something inside Solomon. He had to curb the impulse to pull back. Now wasn't the time to let Rhea's panic rule. He needed to get them to safety.

Solomon lunged when a loud, rending sound came from overhead. He grabbed both kids. Rhea continued her eerie shrieking. Dmitri's eyes rolled. He had a large gash on his head and didn't seem to be aware of what was happening. Solomon hoped he was just not seeing well because of the smoke—he hoped he was wrong and that Dmitri wasn't seriously injured.

But he smelled blood and urine and fear, and it tore him up.

Solomon turned but something had come down over the closet opening. He didn't know what came over him. One second he thought they were all going to die because they were trapped, and the next he simply lost it, setting the kids down and tearing at the inner walls with his hands, kicking and even slamming at them with knees and elbows. They were so close to the outside world, so close to safety, only kept from it by inner walls, insulation, and some two by fours and siding.

He tried to think of Azil and feel him. Azil was there. He was alive.

Then the walls in front of Solomon split. An ax just missed his face.

Solomon said his first curse word. "Shit!" He flopped backwards.

"Sorry," someone called through the opening. "Stay back. Your mate is out here."

"I found them, I found them," Solomon got out, his throat raw, lungs burning. He grabbed a hold of Rhea and Dmitri. Rhea wouldn't stop screaming. Solomon knew the sound of it would haunt him forever. He'd failed in keeping his family safe. It didn't matter what the circumstances were. He'd still failed them.

The wall came down with the help of whoever was trying to tear through it from outside. He stumbled from the burning house with his sister in his arms. Solomon tripped over things—he didn't know what. Hands grabbed at him, keeping him from falling, keeping Dmitri and Rhea from being hurt any further.

Rhea's screaming was cut short, just stopped mid-terror.

"She's passed out. She's alive, Dmitri's alive."

Solomon recognized Azil's voice. His vision was blurry, but he knew that voice. "You're not hurt?"

"Not bad," Azil said. "I got Bobby out but he needs help. So does Sully."

"Dmitri, his head—" Solomon coughed. And coughed. And coughed. He hit the ground, on his knees, retching until he collapsed onto his side. "Gods help us."

"Dmitri will be okay. We all will." Azil pushed some hair off Solomon's brow.

"Solomon!"

Solomon didn't open his eyes, couldn't seem to. They burned, and he was crying too. He knew Adal was beside him, speaking to him.

"You're hurt, oh my gods, how bad?" Adal asked.

"I'll live. You know how I heal." Solomon rubbed at his eyes. That only made it worse. "Azil?"

"Same. I have some burns. Need to shave my hair off, and there are splinters in places I'd rather not mention, but I'll recover. Faster now, thanks to you," Azil added.

"What does that mean?" Adal sounded worried.

Solomon didn't want that. "It means, somehow, when we became mates, I shared my ability to heal faster with Azil."

Adal made a startled noise.

"It's true," Azil added. "Look. Already the smaller places where I was burned are healing. Same as with Solomon."

"That's amazing. I'm so glad for you both." Adal kissed Solomon's cheek. "I'm going to check back in on Rhea and Dmitri. Bobby and Sully need help, too. I wish Remus would hurry up. Or that Rolly was here."

Solomon did too. It seemed even more suspicious to him that Rolly wasn't reachable now. "I think we severely underestimated Tritaya," he muttered.

Azil touched him again, this time on the cheek. "I'm afraid you may be right. It takes an awfully powerful dark magic to do such harm."

"How did the fire start?" Solomon wondered. He pushed himself up to a sitting position. While not healed yet, he already felt somewhat better.

"I don't know." Adal called out, "Hey, Dorso, does anyone know how the fire started?"

"It sounded like thunder, then lightning hit, but the sky's been clear," he replied. "So I'm going with something supernatural, and I hope whoever did it dies a painful, painful death."

"We need to go help Erdwin and the others," Solomon said, fear kicking to roaring life again. "I sent them off into the path of someone more dangerous than I thought. And Remus isn't here yet. We have to go!"

Azil didn't disagree. He was up and running, shifting mid-leap, right alongside Solomon.

Other shifters joined them, sensing the urgency Solomon felt. He wished that reassured him, but the intuitive part of him knew whatever they were facing was much stronger than anything he'd dealt with before. Considering he'd had Bashuan as a father, that was a truly frightening thought.

He yowled, and kept at it until he had the wolf shifters howling out warnings, singing of their war party and deadly intents. That was what Solomon wanted. Let the jaguars and curandera know they were coming. Let them think they had the upper hand.

And maybe they did. But Solomon and his pack had something more going for them — loyalty to one another, and the love of family. Add in a righteous anger that wouldn't be defeated, and they'd be a force to be reckoned with.

They were going to get their shaman, and the rest of their pack. Nothing would stop them.

# Chapter Thirteen

Steven dodged another dart. It struck one of the jaguars instead. He refused to let the drugs take effect. He'd fought off poisons given to him by Bashuan, had survived years of toxic chemicals in his body. A few fucking darts weren't taking him out.

His mates were, as of yet, not tranquilized. They'd killed a few of the jaguars. Now it was time for the asshole with the weapons to go down.

He was bleeding from deep gashes left by the jaguar that had leaped on him. Cole had viciously disemboweled the cat, slinging guts and gore all over. The man's fury was hotter than any Texas summer.

Shaun vibrated with it as well, and had taken down two jaguars. There were still too many of the beasts left, but Solomon was focusing on the armed one who remained in human form. Female or not didn't matter to him. She was dead and just didn't know it.

She raised the tranquilizer gun again. Steven flicked his tail and snarled at her. *Bring it on. I can take more of them.*

He'd never admit it was more luck than skill that had him stumbling aside when she fired. The dart sailed past him. He heard it hit something—not the ground. A check with his mates through their link and he knew they were okay.

Then a wave of power rolled out over the entire area. It was very strong, and Steven was driven to his belly. He recognized the touch of it. Remus had arrived, and Cliff was helping, adding to the already formidable power Remus wielded.

It should have put an end to the fighting. Jaguars yowled. Steven thought some of them died.

But it was all brought to a sudden, frightening halt by the sound of a gunshot ringing out.

"No!" Cliff's shout carried within it a power all on its own.

Steven rolled over and saw Remus, a red spot blooming on his chest, a stunned expression on his face.

*"No!"* Cole wasn't the only one to think it.

Steven couldn't comprehend what was happening until he was the utter devastation on Cliff's face.

*"Shift!"* Steven demanded. Remus had said there was a purpose for Steven, Cole and Shaun being mates. *This had goddamned well better be it. Don't you dare,* Steven seethed at the Fates. *Don't you fucking dare do this!* He didn't care if he was cursed for all of eternity, he'd not stand by and let this happen.

"Good shot, Tritaya," said the woman holding the two weapons.

One older woman floated down from the sky. Probably from the trees, but Steven didn't give a good goddamn. She wasn't an angel. She was the seed of evil itself.

"I believe so," Tritaya said, her voice as dark as her magic. "And my use for you has passed, Wyanem."

"What—?" Wyanem's eyes bulged. She dropped the weapons and grabbed at her throat.

Steven used the distraction to grab his mates. He had Shaun by one hand and Cole by the other. *"Surround them."* He meant Cliff and Remus. His mates knew it. They moved as one to form a triangle around them.

"Stop!" the curandera yelled.

Steven closed his eyes and let his mind flow with his mates. He blocked out the yelling, the building malevolent power around them, and sent their thoughts upward, out toward the broad expanse of the universe, into the arms of the Fates. *"Help us. Help us, damn you!"*

There was an almost physical slap at him. He felt the burn against his cheek, his skin there hot, pained.

*"You do not speak to Us so,"* Lacey said. *"So unwise for one who wants a favor."*

*"A favor? Fuck that! You three witches can't do this! You can't play with our lives like this for your own amusement. Have you no heart at all? None?"* Steven knew he was risking death, eternal damnation, but his fury at the Fates knew no boundaries. *"You give us a few years of happiness, only to destroy us all?"*

*"We are known to be fickle,"* Clo acknowledged. *"Although not as heartless as you seem to believe we are."*

*"Indeed. We'll give you this boon. That is all."* Attie touched a thread, then rubbed a piece of it between her fingers. *"Wake up. It is time."*

The curandera's power was growing. Steven knew a fear unlike any he'd ever experienced. Everyone he loved was at risk. *"The curandera will think she's more powerful than you."*

*"Trying to goad us. Shame, shame."* Clo clicked her tongue. The sound of it hurt Steven's ears. *"Although the boy does have a point. After all, she believes she has taken out our favorite, and by cheating at that. What a total — "*

*"Language,"* Attie said.

And with that, she flicked her wrist.

Steven's brain screamed in agony. The spot on his cheek burned hotter.

A brilliant, white light expanded from his shared consciousness to the actual world as he opened his eyes.

He couldn't describe what happened, not exactly. It was as if an actual portal had been ripped open, from this world to another, or perhaps in time.

When Rolly came through it, he assumed it was a time travel thing given by the Fates.

Rolly looked the same as he had five years ago, except sadness weighed heavily in his eyes. "Dad." He dropped to his knees beside Remus. "No."

Steven left Rolly to his task. He turned and shifted again, running right for the curandera.

Cole and Shaun spread out on either side of him. The queen, Wyanem, was dead, her throat almost flattened. Her eyes bulged and her tongue hung out in a grotesque mask of death.

Tritaya had left whatever weapon she'd shot Remus with elsewhere. She was strong, her magic dark, but she'd expended a great deal of it already. Steven was counting on that to keep him and his loved ones alive.

What he hadn't counted on was the arrival of three of his siblings, and several of Bobby's betas.

That told him very bad things were happening down in the pack dwellings. He could smell smoke and fear on them all.

And he was incensed. He'd had enough of crazy, evil fuckers screwing with his life, with his family and yes, his friends. With his pack.

The curandera aimed a bolt of fire right at Erdwin and the others.

Steven couldn't even yowl, he was so angry. He understood what it meant to see red. He surged forward, already imagining Tritaya's blood on his tongue.

There were still other jaguar shifters alive, and that slowed him down. Steven tore at them without care for himself. He wanted them all dead, dead, dead and out of the way.

Erdwin, Kylie and Elena had avoided being struck by the magic. Steven was relieved for that. He raked his claws down a jaguar's belly, slicing the cat wide open. The wet, lewd slurp of guts spilling out didn't disturb Steven at all. These shifters had come to harm his family. He'd make every one of them pay.

Cole and Shaun were just as violent, killing quickly, coldly. For a while it seemed as if a new jaguar appeared every time they killed one, but eventually, there were only a couple left in front of them. A quick glance around and Steven saw that more jaguar shifters had arrived from somewhere, and he feared for one moment that their reserves were endless.

Shaun bounded over to where there were now over a half dozen more. Those were after Steven's siblings, and the betas. *"Help him, Cole. I have these two."*

Cole leaped right onto the back of one of the two jaguars facing Steven. *"Now you have one."* Cole tore through the back of the cat's neck, almost completely decapitating it.

Actually, Steven then had none, because the last cat turned tail and ran.

Which left the curandera, who was building her power back up, chanting, her hands raised but fingers curled down, drawing her dark magic up from the core of pitch-black evil.

Steven ran at her but hit an invisible wall. It sent a mighty shock through him, causing every inner part of him to ache. He fell backwards but sprang back up and shook off the pain. The numbness would come. It always did when he was hurt bad enough.

Steven pawed at the ground, trying to dig under the barrier. His claws emitted sparks every time they struck it. He wanted to see how his siblings were doing, but he could feel that his mates had a handle on the situation there.

*"They've seen violence before, and they deserve the chance to make their stand,"* Cole thought. *"Have faith in them. They're doing great."*

Steven hadn't wanted them to have to *do* in the first place.

He couldn't get past the barrier. His paws were bloody from trying. Steven threw his head back and roared as much as he was able.

Then his mates were there at his sides, and on their sides, Elena, Kylie and Erdwin.

An instinct took over in him. Steven shifted, as did the others. He once again joined hands with his mates. The six of them, siblings included, spread out to form a circle around the curandera.

Sharp bolts of magic speared out at them.

"Don't let go," Steven shouted. "No matter what!"

A hand on his shoulder, a voice in his ear — both comforted him.

"Follow me," Rolly said.

Steven didn't ask what that meant.

When Rolly began chanting, it was like Steven could see the words in his head, knew the rhythm of the ancient spell Rolly was weaving.

Voices rose around them, through them, their own, and ones belonging to beings Steven couldn't fathom.

The current of power flowed from Rolly into him, from Steven into Cole and Shaun, and down from them until it was a continuous circle, increasing in strength. Every word added to it, every thought and belief of victory, of the power of good over evil.

Steven had never felt anything like it, not even when he and his mates had stood and challenged the Fates. This was something greater even than that. Something pure and whole and *right*.

*And epic*, he thought, as the curandera shrieked. Her voice wasn't human, but that of ancient evils long kept from the Earth.

In that second, Steven knew things he'd never known before nor would again. There was great, horrible power, dark and so malicious it couldn't truly be wiped away. There was also the opposite of that—a good so true and pure, most mortals couldn't grasp it.

Now was the time for good to conquer. The battle itself was an ancient one. Rolly and Steven, along with his mates and siblings, were only vessels to be used.

Steven gave of himself freely, willing to do whatever it took to put the world back to rights. It couldn't end like the curandera wanted it to. The earth would surely be torn apart, quite literally. Chaos would rule and no one would survive it.

There had to be a balance, the yin and the yang. That meant there'd be an opposite of Remus, of that good, vital power. Hopefully, like Remus did with his magic, whoever held the dark would use it wisely and not strive for world domination. That couldn't happen on either side.

Steven jolted when a fresh wave went through him. He opened his eyes, couldn't see anything but white flashes and stars.

He could hear, though. The curandera was being torn apart from the sound of things. The air carried an acrid scent of death unlike any Steven had experienced before.

The chanting grew louder, then Steven heard it—the metallic glide of metal on metal as a thread was cut by Attie. There was one last, final swell of power then it was gone in an instant.

Steven's strength went with it.

Not only his, but everyone else's as well, except maybe Rolly's. Steven fell. His mates fell. His siblings fell.

But they were all alive and, in fact, Steven's wounds were gone. Completely. He wasn't the one in the family that healed so quickly, and yet, he was whole, without even a hint of soreness.

Except on his cheek, where one of the Fates had slapped him for being mouthy. He could handle that.

It took several minutes before Steven could move, much less speak. He had to try several times before he could roll over. While his wounds were gone, he was still as weak as a newborn, and it was frustrating. His vision was hazy too.

And gods above, who was sobbing so loudly?

Steven couldn't fathom it.

Then he got it. He blinked furiously, terrified that all had been screwed up regardless of what had just transpired.

Finally, he could see, and when he did, his own throat tightened against tears he didn't want to shed.

Cliff had Remus gathered in his arms. The shaman was alive, and Cliff's relief was manifesting itself in loud, raw sobs. Remus kept running his fingers through Cliff's hair, murmuring to him.

Rolly squatted between Steven and them.

"Bobby," Erdwin rasped. "Hurt."

Rolly stood. "It should be safe here. Come home when you are able." He shifted and was gone in the blink of an eye.

For one moment Steven thought he'd done the teleporting thing again, but that wasn't the case. Rolly was just hauling ass, running all out in his wolf form.

"I want to go home," Kylie said. "Let's go home."

Cliff had himself together and he stood, still holding onto Remus. "Let's go take care of our alpha."

Remus smiled. "Rolly's going to beat us to it. He's grown quite powerful since he left." He touched his chest where a small white scar now existed. "For what it's worth, I was careless. I didn't think she'd stoop to using a human weapon against me. She covered her strength well. Better than I'd thought possible. I've been schooled by the Fates on growing complacent, and reminded that for all the good, there is equal bad."

"It wouldn't hurt to have the scales tipped to the side of good," Steven groused. His cheek stung more. Maybe he'd just shut up for now.

"It'd be nice, but not the way things work." Remus tilted his head to one side, a far-off look on his face.

"We need to go," Cliff said. "One of your brothers is hurt. Dmitri. Rhea is locked inside her head. Rolly isn't as powerful as Remus, despite what happened here. He'll need help, and I don't think the Fates will intervene for us again."

Steven was already running before Cliff had finished babbling.

# Chapter Fourteen

Azil felt his mate's worry and fear. He tried to remain calm in return, thinking only positive things.

But when a strong, biting, cold wind raked over them, and the sky turned to utter blackness without a single star in sight, Azil knew something very bad was happening.

He heard a gunshot.

*"No, whatever is happening, no,"* Solomon thought.

There was no ignoring the swelling of darkness, not just the absence of light, either, but the rise of an evil that brought to life a hidden sense of terror Azil hadn't known before.

He ran faster, paws slapping the ground, using his back legs to leap great distances.

Solomon was right there with him. They tore up the earth beneath them in their haste to reach the epicenter of where all the magic was coming from.

It was the longest ten minutes of Azil's life. At first Azil couldn't make sense of what he saw.

Tritaya, the curandera, was suspended in the air, pulling up the black magic from below.

A circle of people surrounded her. Dead jaguars littered the area beyond them.

And Cliff held onto Remus, who was clutching at him in return.

Still a good distance away, he could hear the chanting. It brought him to a halt, as it did Solomon. They shifted and both men tipped their head back and closed their eyes. Azil felt it all with his mate, their minds reaching out to those of the people surrounding Tritaya.

It all came to them in a moment, the fighting, the Fates, the gunshot—and death. Rolly's appearance, made possible by the Fates themselves.

Now it was time for the good to gather, the power of that clean, brilliant light to break through.

Azil spoke words he didn't know. He simply opened his mouth and let them out, his voice joining with Solomon's—their combined voices, with those closer to the curandera.

Azil sank to his knees. He knew the instant when it was over, when the evil force was held back, placed back where it belonged. Pieces of it would remain, just as pieces of the good. It was the way of the world, and he understood that when he hadn't before. There was a sacred balance, and upsetting that had dire repercussions. It was why no one would succeed in an attempt to dominate the world.

Cliff's sobs were heart-rending, but at least Remus was okay now.

"It would have destroyed the pack to lose him," Solomon whispered. "Gods, I'm so weak."

Azil opened his eyes. "They are, too. Everyone's on his or her back."

"Maybe it's not as draining on us since we weren't as close." Solomon groaned as he got to his feet. "That was something incredible to be a part of. I feel like my conscience has been expanded."

"I agree. We should head back. They'll be coming along right behind us," Azil said.

They shifted and ran back to the house, or what was left of it. Bobby and Sully needed help, Sully more than Bobby. The wound Bobby had was gruesome but it wouldn't kill him immediately. Sully was barely breathing.

Dmitri had a steady pulse, though it wasn't as strong as Azil would have liked.

Rhea had gone silent, her eyes wide and unfocused. At least she was letting the twins hold her and comfort her.

Azil followed Solomon's lead. When Solomon shifted, so did he. Their wounds were already gone.

"Should we— What should we do?" Azil asked.

Solomon scratched at his burnt hair. "I don't know. I don't know how to help."

Azil stepped closer to him. "What did you do before, before you were here, in this house, with your family?"

Solomon stood up a little taller. "I took care of my family." He nodded once. "Right. Time to do that now."

Rolly arrived seconds before Steven, Shaun and Cole. Behind them came Remus and Cliff, then Erdwin, Elena, Kylie and the betas. In the distance, from where they'd come, Azil saw another fire, this one with lower flames. He shuddered.

"It was the only way to cleanse the area."

He glanced to his side and saw Rolly.

Rolly gave him a gentle smile. "Azil. I'm Rolly. Welcome home."

"Welcome home to you," Azil said, not entirely sure he didn't sound like an idiot. "Thank you."

"You'll do fine here." Rolly shook his hand then released it. "Let me see what I can do for Dmitri and Rhea."

Azil and Solomon stayed with Rolly while he treated both children. Dmitri didn't wake up, but his pulse felt stronger.

"He'll need to be brought to the house, where I can care for him properly. His injury isn't life-threatening now, but he needs certain herbs and rituals I can only do there." Rolly rubbed the small of his back. "I must say, I wish I had the kind of power the Fates lent me while facing Tritaya. I'm grateful for what they've done, though. I was…trapped. Without them, I'd not have been able to come here." Then he glanced off beyond Azil. "Steven, Cole and Shaun are pretty powerful when they meld just right. That was something to experience, having them demand my presence. Shook me out of the cold."

Rolly stood and went to Rhea without further explanation. He knelt and began talking to her quietly.

Azil watched him work, wishing he had a gift like that, a way to help others. He didn't want it for himself, but to be able to give and be of use.

"*Perhaps,*" he heard in an almost-cackle in his head. Gods, had he just bargained with the Fates?

Solomon took his hand. "They aren't evil, or good. They just *are*."

Azil thought he might prefer that the hand holding the scissors of his life string lean more on the side of good than bad. "It's just a thought. I want to help."

"That's how a calling begins, I'd think." Solomon tugged him closer. "We're going to have to build a new home, quickly, too. How are you with tools?"

"Skilled," Azil was happy to announce. Then he watched in awe as Rolly got Rhea talking, the little girl crying and throwing herself into his arms.

"He's so much like his father," Solomon observed.

Azil could see that, though Rolly didn't have the white hair. Instead, his was brown, almost black.

"Ah! God damn it! That hurts!" Bobby shouted, and he sounded mad enough to deck someone.

"It'll hurt more if I jab my finger in it, so be still," Cliff snarled.

Remus shook his head and kept moving his hands in slow circles above the gaping wound.

Cliff continued to give Bobby a hard time. "Quit being a baby and let Remus get it healed enough that we can wrap it. I'll find you a lollipop for after if you're a good boy. Sully didn't whine this much when Remus was fixing him up."

Bobby huffed but quit hollering.

"It looks like everyone will be okay," Azil said.

Rolly continued to soothe Rhea.

Remus finished up with Bobby. "Wrap it tight, Cliff. Wouldn't want it to get infected."

"You sadistic…" Bobby hissed and Remus patted him on top of the head.

"Let's see if anyone else needs tending to," Rolly said a moment later after handing Rhea to Solomon. "I'll borrow Azil, if that's okay with you, Solomon? And you, of course, Azil."

"He makes his own decisions," Solomon replied, a simple look letting Azil know it was truly up to him.

"I'd like that." Azil followed Rolly around to check on the others. There were some small burns and scratches, splinters and such, but no one had been seriously injured besides Sully, Bobby and Dmitri.

"Sully's healed?" Azil asked.

Rolly shook his head. "Oh, not fully, no. He's just not going to die now. He'll have to be kept at the house, too. Either mine or Dad's. Probably Dad's since mine has sat empty for years and will be lacking in supplies. Dmitri will be there, too. He and Rhea have really grown since I've been gone."

A look Azil couldn't interpret crossed Rolly's face.

"I've been gone for most of the years they've been here," Rolly continued. "Not all of them. I came back a few times. I... I missed my home. It's good to be back."

"Why did you leave?" Azil asked. "It doesn't sound like you wanted to go."

Rolly's smile was a sad one. "Reasons I can't explain yet. The timing still isn't right, but I have to be here now. I just hope it doesn't make things too difficult for her."

Azil stopped himself from asking who. He had a feeling that was another thing Rolly couldn't share.

"So, you think you'd like to be a healer?" Rolly said as they resumed walking. "There are different kinds of shamans, you know. Some heal, some curse, some do everything or nothing, only serve themselves. Some kill and protect their packs that way. It just depends on the calling. Are you called?"

Azil stumbled over his own toes. "I— How would I know?"

Rolly stopped walking and pressed a hand over Azil's chest, right above his heart. "You listen here."

Azil closed his eyes and felt it, that warm, hopeful thing that wanted. "Yes. I want to help."

"Then you will." Rolly removed his hand. "We'll start your training after the house gets rebuilt, though. I think we'll all be very busy with that for a few weeks at least."

Azil had never felt so much like he belonged somewhere.

* * * *

Solomon cradled Rhea against his chest. "I'm so glad you're okay, sweetie."

"Dmitri's hurt," Rhea whispered. "He wanted me to come out of the closet but I kept hiding and he got hurt."

"It's not your fault." In fact, Solomon knew part of it was his fault. He'd never thought to come up with a fire safety plan. He doubted many shifters did. "We're all going to sit down once our new home is built, and we'll discuss what to do in case of a fire and other emergencies. Dmitri will be fine. Rolly and Remus will take care of him. In fact, Dmitri is going to stay with Rolly for a little while so Rolly can make sure he's healed up properly."

"Rolly's nice. He's sad. Why is he sad?" Rhea sniffed and rubbed at her nose. "My eyes feel achy."

"He is nice, and I don't know why he's sad. I think maybe he missed his home and his people. He's back now, though, so maybe he'll be happy again." Solomon touched Rhea's nose. "As for your eyes, let's ask if rinsing them out with water will help."

It did help. Rhea's eyes were red from the smoke, but she was healthy, healed.

"I know you'd prefer to keep everyone together, but there's not a big enough house for y'all," Cliff said. "I guess when you first got here, there were tents set up or whatever. Pack's worn out tonight. Actually it's almost morning. Anyway, there are lots of offers from pack members to take some of y'all in until we can set up somewhere for y'all to fit in together. More tents, I guess."

"It was motor homes, and—" Solomon took a step that scared him. He wasn't good at letting go, not at all. "And okay. We can do that. If you'll point out who I need to talk to about where kids can sleep."

Cliff clapped him on the back. "Good man. Just go right over there and talk to that group of people watching us. They're all scared you were gonna say no."

Solomon had been very unfair to the pack. He would make up for it, somehow. Starting with being honest. He strode over to them and bowed his head. "Thank you. I know I've been, ah, standoffish. I really didn't know that until just recently. I was afraid of losing anyone." He raised his head. "You all have showed me how wrong I was. Thank you again. We—I—would be grateful for a place to shelter my family. And I'm very, very grateful for all you have done to help us."

A short, round, older man stepped out of the group. He had messy gray hair and watery eyes. "Son, pride's a good thing to have and all, but it sure can cause us men to miss out on good things."

"Not just you men, George," a woman added. "Us ladies aren't perfect." She grinned. "We just look like we're perfect. I'm Udia. I have a spare room with a double bed in it."

Soon Solomon had a place for everyone. He and Azil would stay with Rolly and Dmitri. Rhea wanted to be with Dmitri but for now, Remus and Cliff were okay with taking her in.

"We'll put her to work," Cliff promised.

"I'll work. I will." Rhea yawned. "Can I sleep first?"

Cliff might be a sarcastic jerk at times, but he melted under that request. "Yeah, you sure can. Sleep as long as you want to."

"'Kay." Rhea looked at Solomon. "Hug."

Solomon could do that.

"Azil too," Rhea said, gesturing at him.

"Someone has y'all wrapped around her finger." Cliff held up a hand. "Don't even. I already know I'm next."

Solomon chuckled and slipped an arm around Azil's waist. "Sweet dreams, Rhea."

Erdwin came over. "Solomon, I don't know about this. I'm— You know how I am around people."

Solomon looked Erdwin in the eyes. "You can do this. I've kept all of us away from the pack when I shouldn't have. Learn from my mistake, little bro. See if you can make friends of these people who want to help us. Don't be scared like I was." *Still am, but it's time to grow up.* "You can come stay with us at Rolly's if—"

"No, no." Erdwin backed up, waving his hands in front of him, eyes huge. "I'll try with Grace and her family. She, um. She's nice."

Solomon was puzzled. "And Rolly isn't?"

Erdwin turned tail and ran.

"That's just weird," Solomon mused to Azil. Then he sighed so heartily it almost hurt. "Gods, I'm so glad everyone's okay. It could have been so much worse." He turned to look at what remained of the house. "This, it's just a thing. I mean, it's the first real, secure home we had, but it's still just a thing. What I know is, home isn't necessarily a place. It's the people. It's really where the heart is, like that old saying. And my heart, it's with you and my family."

Azil cuddled in and pressed a kiss to Solomon's neck. "Now I know what home is. The clan, that was a miserable way to live. Do you think Bobby will still go after them?"

"I don't know, but I think I need to go back. If there's something of my mother's there, even a picture or a note, I'd like to have it for me and my siblings." Solomon groaned. "I wish we'd have planned a way to get a hold of Leeloo. Dang it, I didn't even think of it."

"Well, if we go back, maybe she'll be ruling the clan by then. Someone will take it over, and I'm hoping it will be her and she'll be fair." Azil worried his lower lip with his teeth.

"She'd be fair, I think," Solomon said. He pressed a thumb to Azil's lip. "Stop. You'll make it bleed. Let me get Dmitri, then we'll see if Rolly's ready. He was checking up on Bobby and Sully with Remus a minute ago."

Azil started them in that direction. "They're all done. Remus has people helping him get Sully to the house."

"Good. I want to shower until I don't reek, then lie down with you and sleep for a good eight hours." Solomon liked the way he and Azil companionably bumped shoulders and occasionally hips as they walked.

"Do you need us to help move Sully?" Azil asked when they reached Remus and the others.

With Bobby's arm injured, he wouldn't be able to lift Sully. Bobby looked like he was pouting over that, too.

"We've got him, but thank you." Remus counted to three, then helped the betas lift Sully. "Sturdy young man. He'll be just fine, Bobby."

Rolly watched them leave. "Well, that leaves us. Shall we? I can't promise that the house isn't musky from being closed up. Dad said he aired it out once a week, so maybe it won't be awful. Clean sheets might be a challenge."

"I don't care if the sheets are covered in dust, I just want to make sure Dmitri is comfortable, then shower before I go to sleep," Solomon said. He looked at his brother, sleeping peacefully in his arms. "He's going to be okay."

"He'll be just fine. He's healing even now. Let me ask you this, though. Why shower if you don't care about the bed being dirty?" Rolly teased. "Just go to bed like you are."

"I don't want to smell the smoke." Solomon remembered his singed hair. "And if you have some scissors or clippers, I'd like to take the burnt parts of my hair off, too."

"Me too." Azil grimaced. "I think mine's going to have to go down to nothing. There's a patch back here where I can feel scalp."

Solomon checked. "Yeah, that's probably where you had an actual burn but it healed. Should be good to grow new hair." He rubbed the bald spot. "You're going to be hot with a shiny scalp. All disciplinarian looking."

"Ahem." Rolly cleared his throat. "That may be too much information for me, guys. By all means, have sex and enjoy each other while staying with me, but I would rather not have the image of what you just described in my head. Now I see Azil wielding one of those floggers and—"

"And *that's* too much info," Solomon declared. "Jeez, Rolly, you dirty-minded shaman! Thank goodness Dmitri is snoozing."

"I wouldn't have joked, otherwise, Solomon." Rolly chortled, his gray eyes crinkling around the outer edges. "Well, I have always had a very active imagination, and you started it with the whole hot disciplinarian thing. And just to clarify, should you ever wonder, I am *not* into floggers."

Solomon eyed Rolly. "You know that for a fact?"

Rolly smirked. "Yes, I do."

"Huh." It just went to show that one shouldn't judge a book by the cover, though it was always tempting. "So, who wielded the flogger? You might screech about TMI but I'm curious."

"You'll just have to keep wondering. I've never kissed and told."

Oh, Rolly was kind of evil on the inside. Solomon pointed at him. "That's not kissing. That's the kind of stuff that's going to be a big Hollywood movie soon."

Rolly frowned at him. "What in the world are you talking about?"

"You've been away too long." Solomon was going to have fun filling Rolly in on some of the changes in the world.

*Later.* Right then, all he wanted was to curl up and rest in the comforting arms of his mate.

# Chapter Fifteen

Solomon woke suddenly to a sweet, erotic heat and constricting muscles that cocooned his shaft perfectly, fully.

He blinked away the sleep from his eyes and propped up enough to see what was happening. "Oh, more wake-ups like this one, please," he rasped as Azil continued to suck his dick.

Azil winked at him, at the same time flicking that agile tongue around Solomon's slit. Then he went down, taking more of Solomon's length into his mouth.

It was perfect and beautiful. Solomon's head swam with pleasure. When Azil swallowed, Solomon's heart tried to break right out of his chest. His balls drew tight as he hovered at the edge, needing something more to send him flying.

*"Can I touch you?"* Azil asked silently, brushing a fingertip over Solomon's pucker.

Solomon groaned and flopped back. "Yes, please. I want to know how it feels."

Azil came back up to tongue his frenulum. He then breached his hole with the tip of a slick digit, while at the same time diving back down on Solomon's cock.

Solomon came apart from the inside out as rapturous sensations spiraled from his hole to his balls and out his cock.

All Solomon could do was moan and writhe, and clutch at the sheets as he rode out his release. When he stopped trembling, Azil was kneeling beside him, masturbating frantically.

Solomon grabbed his hips and tugged.

Azil looked like he wanted to argue, but his need was too intense to turn away Solomon's offer. He straddled Solomon's chest and angled his dick downward.

Solomon opened his mouth, eager, wanton.

Then it was Azil who whimpered as his broad cock pushed into Solomon's mouth. His heavy balls rested below Solomon's chin before Azil pulled his length back out. "Gods," he rasped, spearing a hand through Solomon's hair. "I—"

"Do it," Solomon willed him. "Do it."

Azil tightened his grip on Solomon's hair and used that hold to raise his head. Then he began to move his hips in short, quick thrusts that never penetrated Solomon's throat.

Solomon sealed his mouth tightly around the shaft, so tightly that soon his lips hurt from covering his teeth. He sucked, his jaw beginning to ache, but he didn't want Azil to stop.

Azil grunted every time he pushed in. His eyes had a glazed, hungry look. Azil's expression was stark, bordering on pained as he chased his release.

Solomon flicked his tongue over every bit of Azil's cock he could reach. He ran his hands up Azil's thighs and farther back until he cupped Azil's cheeks. Then he squeezed, kneading Azil's butt.

Azil's skin was sheened with sweat as he thrust into Solomon's mouth faster. His need flowed into Solomon, so great that it hurt.

Solomon let his fingertips graze over Azil's hole. He scraped that tender skin gently, and Azil bucked. He drove his cock in deeper than he had before, hips jerking roughly as spunk hit Solomon's tongue.

He drank eagerly as Azil panted and thrust.

Then Azil was moving down his body, his wet cock leaving a trail down Solomon's chest.

Solomon's lips felt swollen and hot, but Azil's mouth was on his, his tongue sliding in. Solomon knew he had to be tasting himself, and that knowledge almost had his cock perking back up. Had he not just come, he might have rolled Azil onto his stomach and taken him.

Although, his cock hadn't gone soft yet. "Azil…"

"Anything, Solomon. Anything. I want you happy," Azil said. "Did you like it when I touched your hole?"

Solomon caught a clue. "You interested in that, Az? In making love to me? Putting that fat, pretty cock of yours up my butt?" Solomon groaned. "Ugh. I may have to start cussing for some things. That just doesn't sound as sexy as asking if you'd like to fuck my ass."

Azil whimpered.

Solomon sat up, bracing his back against the headboard. "You like that idea a whole lot. I do, too. We need to check on Dmitri first."

"I already did," Azil said. "You were so tired, you didn't even wake up when I got out of bed. It's early afternoon now, and…" He sighed. "We should wait for any more of this between us." He gestured from himself to Solomon. "I'm starving, and we have house plans to go over, and Dmitri will want to see you."

"He's awake?" Solomon was already out of bed. "He's okay?"

"He still has a bit of a headache, but even the cut is healed up. Either he has your healing powers or Remus and Rolly, and Cliff, really did some special stuff to him." Azil eyed Solomon. "I need to rinse off real quick. Meet you in the kitchen?"

"Sure." Solomon grinned. He was happy, so happy considering the week he'd had. But he had his mate, and his family was all alive and healing, if not already well. There was no reason for him not to be happy. "Do you mind if I take care of a few things in the bathroom while you shower? Save on time and all that."

"Er, I don't mind. I might peek past the shower curtain." Azil blushed when he said it.

The man was entirely too handsome for his own good, and the fact that he hadn't a clue about that only added to his allure.

Solomon caught him peeking quite often in the bathroom, but he was doing some ogling himself. He even went so far as to pull the shower curtain back and to ask Azil to masturbate for him.

Azil moved the showerhead out of the way so the water didn't fall on him. "Okay. I can do that."

"Imagine me fingering your hole. Slick up a couple of fingers and—" Solomon stopped, wanting to do that himself. He also wanted to watch Azil pleasure himself, so he was torn.

Azil wasn't. He pushed two thick fingers into his pucker. "Ahh, gods." He started jacking off with fast, wet strokes.

"So gorgeous," Solomon murmured. "Look at that big cock. I want that in me, Az. I want to feel it spreading me open, feel your cum in me."

Azil cried out, spunk jetting up and splattering on his stomach and hand.

"That was absolutely the hottest thing I've ever seen. Right up there with the way your mouth looks stretched around my cock, and the way your hole grips my dick, and…" Solomon chuckled. "You're just all kinds of sexy, Azil."

Azil shuddered. "You need?"

"This will keep." Solomon palmed his hard shaft. "I'm in the mood for a little anticipation. Let it build up until tonight, when you've got me spread out on the bed, stretched open." *Hmm. Maybe I'm not so bad at talking dirty, and who says talking dirty has to be…dirty? It can just be hot.*

Azil looked down at his own cock, softening in his grip. "I'll hopefully last longer than ten seconds, since I've come twice already."

Solomon snorted. "You'll last longer than that." He finished up in the bathroom then dressed in some clothes he found on top of the dresser.

"Rolly gave me those earlier. He said people are bringing clothes and other things for us, and leaving them at the ceremonial center." Azil beamed. "You have a wonderful pack."

"We," Solomon corrected. "We have a wonderful pack."

* * * *

Dmitri looked almost a hundred percent better. He complained of a headache, but once Rolly made him drink some pungent brown tea, Dmitri dozed off.

"Sleep is what he needs now." Rolly patted Dmitri's arm. "He's a good kid. Rhea's already been here to check on him. I think she wants to sleep in the same room with him. Cliff might be heartbroken."

"Who'd have thought that? You think Cliff and your dad will have more kids? Adopt or, I don't know. Conjure one?" Solomon joked.

Rolly narrowed his eyes and pointed at him. "That's not funny. My youngest brother is already the spawn of Satan. Pretty sure he was conjured. They can adopt. There are plenty of pups needing homes. There's even an orphanage of sorts in Colorado. One of the many things I learned while traveling around."

"Are you ever going to tell me why you left?" Solomon asked. He wasn't exactly best friends with Rolly, but they had an easy camaraderie.

"No. At least, not for a while." Rolly stood from where he'd been sitting on the edge of the bed. "I'm going to move the smaller futon in here for Rhea. Care to help?"

"I will," Azil volunteered. "I'll move it and someone else can make it up. I hate putting sheets on."

"Guess that leaves me with sheet duty." Solomon found the twin-size sheets and in short order they had a place for Rhea ready.

Solomon moved on to the next item he needed to deal with. "We need to get the family together, at least the older ones if we can, and if Bobby's available, see what we can come up with for building another home."

"Bobby's probably at Remus' still, if you want to go next door and chat with him?" Rolly suggested. "I'll stay here in case Dmitri wakes up. I'd think you could fit all the family and everyone helping to build the house over at the ceremonial grounds. Put up a few folding tables, grab some chairs. It should work even though y'all will be outside."

"That's a great idea, Rolly, thanks." Solomon and Azil left and walked to Remus and Cliff's house.

When Remus answered, it was obvious the man wasn't suffering any lingering effects of almost dying, or perhaps dying completely. Solomon wasn't going to ask if Remus had passed from the mortal realm for any period of time before being brought back to full health.

"Come in. Cliff is playing dolls with Rhea—"

"Remus!" Cliff barked. "You— Don't tell people that!"

Solomon entered the living room just in time to see Cliff cram a doll behind his back.

He glared belligerently at Solomon. "What? You don't play with her?"

Solomon tried not to laugh but wasn't very successful.

"Solomon plays dolls with me, and Erdwin plays makeup with me. They don't hide," Rhea scolded. "Dmitri plays wrestling and tag with me. He only hides when I'm 'It'."

"I'm new to playing, so cut me some slack, kiddo. And hand me those red boots for Marcy here." Cliff trotted the doll out. "She's a *supermodel-doctor-astronaut*. My girl can do it all."

He looked about as proud as a man could when playing with dolls.

Solomon gave him a thumbs-up. "You need some kids, Cliff. May six or seven."

"Don't make me thump you," Remus said from behind him. "Six or seven. We can discuss one or two."

Cliff's smile lit up his whole face. It was kind of creepy. "We can?"

Remus thumped Solomon anyway. "You and Azil will have an even dozen."

Solomon's jaw dropped as he turned and gawped at the shaman.

So did Azil's.

Solomon got it together first. "Tell me that wasn't a curse."

Remus laughed.

"Remus." Solomon only whined a little.

"Of course it's not a curse, Solomon." Remus cupped his shoulder.

Solomon almost sagged with relief.

Remus gave him a little squeeze. "It's a blessing."

"Aw, crap." Solomon considered that then decided he was good with it. "Thanks for the heads-up. Now we can really plan for a new house."

"Part of why I told you." Remus placed his other hand on Azil's shoulder. "Are you okay, son?"

"Twelve?" Azil squeaked.

Remus nodded. "If it helps, three of them will be the same age, from the same litter."

Solomon immediately imagined bottles and multiple middle-of-the-night feedings. "We'll never get any sleep then."

"Y'all ain't gonna get any sleep ever again if you wake Sully up," Bobby muttered as he came into the room. "Seriously. Who made the sound like a mouse gettin' stepped on?"

Azil raised his hand.

Bobby huffed. "Well, stop it or I'll have to yank your squeaker out."

Azil's eyes rounded then narrowed.

Bobby grinned. "Wanna try me, kitty boy?"

Azil pursed his lips like he was considering it.

Solomon knew what was going on in his mate's head. He wasn't worried.

Bobby's amusement darkened just a tad. "Aw, come on now, I'd think Solomon's mate would have more sense than that!"

Azil snickered.

Bobby glared. "Think you're funny, huh?"

"Are you still going after the Vento clan?" Azil asked.

Bobby cocked a hip and planted a fist on it. "You're just tryin' to throw me off, but it ain't gonna work, kitty. And yeah, I gotta make sure there won't be any more of this bullshit with kidnapping my pack members."

"Bobby said a bad word!" Rhea shouted gleefully, clapping her hands. "He has to do the laundry!"

Bobby leaned to the left to peer around Azil and Solomon. "Nuh-uh, sweets. The alpha is exempt."

Rhea got up and ran over to stand in front of Bobby. She crossed her thin arms over her chest. "That's not fair. Solomon says everyone has to follow the rules, it's only fair and good people do what's right. It's not right to cuss around me or any little kid. If you don't follow the rules then you're bad. Are you bad, Bobby?"

"In the best way," he said with a purr. "But obviously not the kinda bad you're worried about because it looks like I'll be doing the da—er, danged laundry. Sheesh."

"Good save," Cliff called out. "You have laundry next Wednesday. I've got it until then."

"Only a week? You're becoming a prude, Cliff." Bobby laughed so loud he woke Sully. "Aw, man.

Now I'm the one waking my man." But he looked happy when he turned and ran off to Sully's room.

"I hope he's not planning on going on that trip until after we've got the house built." Solomon frowned. "Though I guess, if he does, we can go anyway, as long as the plans are drawn up and everything's set to be done."

"He'll want to wait until Sully's up to snuff. Probably a couple of weeks." Remus gestured toward Sully's room. "He was as close to death as anyone I've had to work with before. Barring being completely dead, and as the movie *The Princess Bride* explains, there are different kinds of dead."

Solomon caught just the slightest of shudders going over Remus. He wondered if Remus had been one of those kinds of dead.

"We need to talk to Bobby. Think he'll have a cow if we go into Sully's room?" Solomon asked.

"Should be fine. Sully will probably appreciate the company." Remus waved them off. "Rhea, let's see what we can find to dress Cliff up in, hmm?"

"Remus, I swear—" Cliff growled.

Solomon and Azil went after Bobby. They had a house to design and an alpha to bug.

# Chapter Sixteen

"This is not my idea of a vacation, you jerk," Elena grumbled as they slashed their way through the dense foliage. "And I don't ever want to get on an airplane again once we get home. I prefer my feet to be firmly on the ground."

"Stop whining, El. This is cool!" Jerek exclaimed. He swatted at a bug. "Even the insects are pretty."

Keno shrieked. "I hate bugs! And I'm with El, I'm never getting on a plane again after we get home."

Jerek stopped tromping along and stared at his twin. "Well, how the heck are we going to Hawaii and all those other places in the world?"

"By ship or yacht or shipping crate," Keno grumbled. "Any way but flying."

"You just need to relax and take a nap. That's what I did on the plane." Jerek resumed walking.

Elena shook her head. "You two are more entertaining than anything on TV."

"I think they're too noisy," Bobby said. "And we all oughta shift before we get eaten alive by skeeters and other hungry bugs out here."

"He has an excellent idea," Remus agreed. "Sully, your mate is intelligent at times."

Sully patted Bobby's butt. "I'll keep him."

Short of a slight limp and a scar running from the back of his right ear to the nape of his neck, Sully had no lingering signs of the injuries that had almost ended his life.

Solomon was glad. Bobby and Sully deserved to be happy, not hurting. So did he and Azil, and everyone else in the pack.

"Alpha, are we shifting?" Cordelia, one of the betas, asked.

"Sure, that's what I said, wasn't it?" Bobby whipped off his shirt. "Well, I want Geo and Naya to take our clothes back to the jet and wait there. We should be back by tomorrow at the latest."

"Yes, Alpha." Geo and Naya gathered up the clothing and shoes before heading to the plane.

Bobby shifted first, and everyone else followed suit.

Solomon thought the rainforest was lovely, but he had no desire to be there any longer than necessary. Three weeks and a couple of days had passed since the fire, and the house was coming along quickly. He wanted to get back and make it into a home for his family.

But he knew home *was* his family, and his mate, and the pack. Family—he would do what he could to find any family members, not just mothers, for his brothers and sisters. There was a lot of research to be done.

*"I will help you. We can do this together, and the older kids, they'll help, I bet."*

Azil's support warmed Solomon's heart. *"Thank you."*

Solomon was learning that he could love greatly, and still let go. It didn't mean any of his siblings would be gone forever. It just meant they were turning into strong, independent adults who needed to live their own lives.

He tried not to get down about it, but he did fret that he was still too clingy.

A brilliant, blue bird flew in front of them not a dozen feet ahead. The beauty of it distracted Solomon from his thoughts. He began to pay more attention to his surroundings, the scents, sounds and sights of it. Even the feel of the ground beneath the pads of his feet. Short of being kidnapped, he'd never been far from wherever he'd lived, be it chained up in a filthy room on Bashuan's property, or at the pack lands outside of San Antonio.

Maybe he needed to try to enjoy this little adventure.

*"That's the spirit. This is truly a beautiful place to be. I love Texas, don't get me wrong, but it's so dry there. I miss the rains."* Azil turned his nose up and sniffed. *"Smell."*

Solomon did and scented the rain coming. It hit them a minute later, fat, heavy drops pelting them. It felt wonderful.

Solomon bounded through it, chuffing, feeling playful. Soon he had even the betas chasing tails and acting like a bunch of pups and kittens. It was fun.

When the rain stopped, Solomon and the others calmed down and went back to heading for the Vento clan's lands. Azil led most of the way there, with Bobby, Sully and the betas moving to the front when they reached the outskirts of the property.

Bobby, never shy to begin with, let out a loud series of howls and barks announcing their presence. There were no wolves native to the area, so the racket was sure to send creatures everywhere scattering.

Except for a pack of jaguars, sleek, deadly, their golden fur dotted with black rosettes.

Azil shoved his way to the front. Solomon went with him.

Bobby nipped at them both, but let them stand beside him in the end.

One jaguar slunk forward. She smelled familiar to Solomon. He wrinkled his nose and chuffed.

A second female joined her.

Solomon leaned against Bobby.

Bobby flicked him with his wolfie tail. It was a 'go ahead' as far as Solomon was concerned.

He shifted, Azil doing the same.

The two jaguars morphed into Leeloo and a stunning woman with dark skin and pale green eyes.

"Glad you two survived," Leeloo said, smiling.

Solomon thought it might have been the first time he'd seen her do that. "We did. Tritaya and Wyanem are dead. Lots of other jaguar shifters that were with them, too."

Bobby shifted then. "Yeah, they were stupid. Are you?"

Leeloo looked him up and down then arched an eyebrow at Solomon and Azil.

"Our alpha, Bobby," Azil explained by way of introduction. "He's very blunt."

"Blunt is fine. This is Shani, my mate. She is everything."

Shani nodded, appearing pleased.

Then Leeloo focused on Bobby. "Do I look like I'm stupid? I stayed here and took over the clan. The ones who went after you and yours, they're all dead." Then she looked at the other shifters. "Please tell me you brought your shaman."

Remus' white fur almost glowed, it was so bright. He shifted and approached Leeloo. "Of course I came. I'm needed."

"And where he goes, I go." Cliff stood behind Remus.

Leeloo frowned. "You aren't just a wolf."

"Perceptive." That was all Cliff said.

Leeloo harrumphed but let it go. "Alpha Bobby, have you come in peace? We do not look to start a war. We only want to live our lives peacefully here in the jungle."

"As long as y'all don't start shit, we'll do just fine. And also, any information you might have about Solomon's mom, that'd be great." Bobby shifted then yipped.

"Guess he's ready for us to get a move on," Cliff said.

"How is your brother, Lotu?" Azil asked Leeloo.

She averted her gaze. "He's not good. I think he's dead—inside I mean. He reacts to nothing. Getting food into him—he doesn't want to be here anymore, but I can't just let him go like that."

"Perhaps I can help him," Remus murmured. "A broken soul takes time and much meditation and prayers to help mend. If he will come back with us, and you'll allow that."

"Anything," Leeloo vowed. "Anything that will help him. Thank you." To Solomon, she said, "And you. I do have some things I've found in Wyanem's belongings. I knew she was dead. Same with the curandera. The whole encampment suddenly felt like a dark veil had been lifted almost a month ago."

"That'd be it." Solomon was glad Leeloo had gone back. She looked a lot better, no longer drawn and worn. "We'll follow." He shifted, as did the others. Bobby took the lead with Sully. Everyone else filed in behind them.

In the encampment, huts were set up in a rectangular pattern. About twenty-five of them, all well taken care of. In the center of the area was a deep fire pit. Solomon guessed it was ceremonial. It didn't look as if it'd been used in a long time.

Shifters in jaguar and human forms watched them approach. Solomon noted that there were only a few males in the clan.

*"I think they all fled when given the chance. It wouldn't be likely that most would trust a woman from the guard telling them they were free. Not for long, so they'd run before she could change her mind. It's what I would have done,"* Azil explained.

A familiar yowl caused Solomon to stop and crane his neck. He saw Elena standing nose to nose with a female jaguar. They were sniffing, then they were licking. Solomon started to run over to find out what was going on.

Azil slid in front of him. *"Solomon..."*

*"What is it? Why is that jaguar licking my little sister?"* Solomon demanded.

*"Your sister is an adult. Why do you think she'd let some strange cat lick her?"*

Solomon didn't like that question. He didn't like the only answer he could come up with.

Jerek and Keno stopped and made inquisitive noises at Elena. Bobby barked at them all.

Solomon ignored him, watching instead the way the jaguar and Elena leaned toward each other. *"I'm not ready to make this big of a step back. I can't let go so soon."*

*"You might not have to. Welcome Elena's mate to the family. Offer her a home with us. She might come. Elena doesn't care for the insects here, after all."*

As if to emphasize Azil's point, what looked a whole lot like a giant cockroach flew right above Solomon's head.

More than a couple of his pack flipped out, barking, yelping, snarling and swatting.

Elena turned toward the commotion, her eyes huge when she saw the bug.

Maybe Azil was right. Elena and her mate could come live with them, or at least on the pack property. Solomon decided supportive and hopeful was the way to be, so he went over to meet Elena's mate, if it was, indeed, her mate.

It didn't take long for him to know that the jaguar and Elena were meant for each other. The scent of arousal hit him—a repugnant smell, considering part of it belonged to his sister. Solomon settled for a happy, chuffed greeting before he backed away.

Bobby and the others were several yards ahead. Solomon glanced back at Elena and the twins. *Come on,* he mewled. They got the gist of it.

He supposed it was kind of cute the way Elena and the jaguar wound their tails together as they walked.

\* \* \* \*

It was strange to be back with the clan, even though the clan itself was different. Azil still felt uncomfortable there. He wanted to go back to Texas, even if he did miss the rains and the beauty of the jungle. There were too many bad memories here.

"Man, seems weird that there ain't many males left here. I can see why the split, but I gotta wonder where they went." Bobby sat on a stool in the hut they were sharing. Leeloo had put them in two of them, with the betas in their own hut. "And that Luto, he's all kinds of fucked up. Makes me determined to be a better alpha. No leader should screw up their pack like that. This place, it just feels wrong."

Azil took a seat across from Bobby, beside Sully. "Not like it did. I admit, it's not a comfortable place to be, but it isn't nearly as bad as it was. I'm glad Elena and Naniv are coming back with us, though. Even with Remus and Cliff doing a cleansing on this clan and the property, to me it will never be clean."

"I gotta figure out how we're getting that guy back to the plane. He's a zombie. Guess we'll pull him on a pallet or something." Bobby poked at the platter of food on the table. "None of this is meat."

"There is too meat on that platter," Sully argued. "It's just...rodents."

Azil felt his cheeks heat up. "There hasn't been much game in this area for a long time. Couple of years, at least. Tritaya's dark magic kept it away, isn't that what Remus said?"

"Yeah, but she's dead and we need real food." Bobby wrinkled his nose. "I'm not eating any of that. I'll do without until tomorrow. There'll be a bunny or something to eat on the way back, and if not, there's steaks in the jet."

That guaranteed none of the rest of them were going to eat tonight, either. Azil had grown used to food he liked, and he'd been hungry many times when with the clan. He could survive a night of missed meals.

"No one likes our food options, but until we can tempt the wildlife back, we have to make do," Leeloo said as she strode over to join them. "And there're your shamans, Remus and Cliff. They will help us. If we absolutely have to, we can move, but that will almost certainly mean fighting with other shifter clans, and I'd prefer to avoid that. Our numbers have shrunk substantially in the past month."

"Do you think any of the men will come back?" Azil asked her.

Leeloo shook her head. "Why would they? After the way they were treated? I hope every one of them goes on to great happiness. I hope that ability wasn't stolen from them as well." She approached Solomon. "Where are your siblings?"

Solomon called out for Elena, Jerek and Keno. He gestured to the box Leeloo held. "Is that it?"

"All I have found. If there's anything more, I will contact you." She handed the box to him.

Solomon set it on the bar. His siblings gathered around him. He glanced at each of them. "Would one of you prefer to open it?"

"No, you do it. You're the oldest, and...and you've taken care of us like she would have," Elena said.

Jerek and Keno agreed.

Solomon removed the lid and took out the faded photograph on top. "She was beautiful. Looked just like you, Elena." He held the picture up. The young woman in it was smiling confidently at whoever had held the camera. She looked so much like Elena, they could have been twins with their dark hair and eyes, sharp cheekbones and full lips. They even had the same arch to their eyebrows.

"She did," Elena murmured, touching the edge of the photo.

Solomon handed it to her. "We'll make copies. Jerek and Keno, you both have the same shape to your face as she did, and look at Irial's eyes."

Azil could see the resemblance between Solomon and Irial as well. He was a more masculine version of her, and without a doubt Irial's son.

Solomon next took out a journal.

"Your mother's," Leeloo explained. "I think Wyanem was very jealous of your mother. She wasn't beautiful like Irial, and certainly not kind. I don't know if Irial was kind or not, but I think she must have been. Her children are all very good people."

"Thank you." Solomon surprised Leeloo with a hug.

"I'll leave you to your mementos. When you are awake, as a group or singularly, in pairs, whatever, come to our place in the morning. We've got a hook-up to help transport Lotu. I will pull it. You and your pack have done so much for us already." She took a deep breath then blew it out slowly. "Bobby, if I can ever help, please let me know. Between removing the curandera, the queen, and setting this clan free, as well as the cleansing and...and taking Lotu, I cannot ever repay you. Thank you."

Bobby didn't smirk or smart off. He merely nodded and said, "You're welcome. I will."

Leeloo left the hut.

Bobby waggled his eyebrows at Sully. "Let's go to bed so you can distract me from my empty stomach."

Sully laughed and slid off the bar stool. "Works both ways, stud."

"Oh, I'm a stud." Bobby preened and strutted all the way to the largest of the three bedrooms. He winked at them all then shut the door.

Azil sat with Solomon and the others as they went through the box. There weren't many things in there. The picture, journal, a few letters, some scraps of material, and a handful of thin golden bangles.

"Tomorrow I'm going to ask Leeloo if Wyanem kept any journals. There might be more information in them if she did." Solomon put the lid back on the box.

"Come take a walk with me," Azil requested. "I'd like to show you some of the forest."

"Don't wander too far," Cliff advised. "We'll be doing the cleansing in about an hour, too. If you could be in the clan's land by then, that'd be, hmm, wise, I'd say."

Azil took Solomon by the hand. He wasn't going to actually leave the vicinity.

"Where are we really going?" Solomon asked once they were outside.

Azil pointed to a large building set farther back than the others. "There. It's where the males were kept as children, until they were taken, claimed, or like me and a few others, put in with the guards. It should be empty now."

"Empty, huh?" Solomon tucked him in close at his side. "What about bad memories?"

"I don't intend to be thinking once I've got you in there. Not about anything other than your body and all the things I can do to it."

Solomon shivered. "I'm down with that."

Azil sent his mate a smile that he hoped was sexy, not silly. "Good. I wouldn't mind convincing you if I needed to."

"We could role play," Solomon suggested. "Oh, you could be the cop and I'll be the bad boy. I'd rather not get into the teacher-student, daddy-son thing. That'd just kill it for me."

"I was talking about foreplay, but we could certainly do some role-playing." Azil was assuming from what Solomon had just said, it meant pretending to be other types of people. He could so do that.

"Foreplay is good. Foreplay is great, actually. So is lube."

Azil took a small tube from his pocket. "There was some in the hut, in the bathroom. Several of these, actually. Leeloo must have had it prepared ahead of time."

"Leeloo is awesome." Solomon stopped him for a quick kiss. "You're going to make love to me."

"I am." Azil didn't do it often, but he enjoyed it immensely when he topped Solomon.

"Good. I'm so in the mood for that. Your cock in my ass, mmm." Another kiss, this one deeper.

Azil cupped Solomon's bulge while they were at it. He loved the way it was too much for his hand.

"Inside," Azil finally said, a little breathless from the kisses. "Come on." He jogged to the building. The door opened easily. A quick inspection proved the place to be as empty as Azil had hoped.

Azil took them to the set of rooms the monitors had slept in. The beds there were bigger.

He was worn out but also wired, stressed and horny. "We have an hour. I'm not sure Cliff and Remus won't come into the building for the cleansing. There are probably many bad things needing to be wiped out of here. But we're going to start doing that right now." Azil told himself not to be embarrassed. The next part was very important. "With love. I love you, Solomon."

Solomon framed Azil's face with strong, warm hands. "Az, honey, you know I love you, too. So much. I want to give you everything."

"I understand that. It's what I want for you, too." And he knew one way to get started on that. Not that Solomon was unhappy, but Azil could make him feel better. He could make them both feel better. He rubbed his palm over that tempting bulge.

"Think we have enough time?" Solomon whispered against his lips. "I could stay here with you all night and make love to you unceasingly. Think of all the things we could do together."

Azil couldn't help it, he whimpered, need growing in him. "We have an hour. That's plenty of time for what I have in mind. Another night, when we won't get busted by our shaman, we can take as long as we want."

"I'm going to be loud tonight. Everyone will know what we're doing if they're within a hundred yards of us," Solomon warned, backing away with a loose-hipped gait that made his package swivel nicely. He unfastened the buttons of the shirt he'd been lent, and took it off before dropping it on the floor.

Azil backed up until he felt the bed behind him. He put the lube on it, then sat down and watched his mate. Azil parted his legs, his clothing making sitting uncomfortable, then he scooted forward on the bed. His own cock was hard and poking at the sweats confining it, but that could wait. He gripped Solomon's hips as soon as the man was in reach.

"You've got more clothes back in our room?" he asked, letting his breath waft over the tip of Solomon's cock.

Solomon's answer was a strangled sound as he grabbed the back of Azil's head and thrust. Azil did love such eagerness in his mate.

"I'll come too soon," Solomon began, but he wasn't pulling away.

Azil cupped his butt and mouthed the length of his covered cock, leaving a wet path along the material. He raised his head enough to say, "No you won't. You have more control than that."

Azil dipped his head and nosed under Solomon's balls. The musky, earthy scent of the man was addictive. He found the button on his pants and undid it, then slid the zipper tab down.

Bare skin—Solomon hadn't bothered with briefs or, more likely, hadn't been given any. There'd been none in Azil's pile of clothing. Azil took out the thick cock and gave it a loving stroke. He had to stop sniffing around Solomon's balls long enough to let him get the pants down, then Azil was right back at them.

"Here," Solomon offered, hooking one leg over Azil's shoulder. "Is it too much weight?"

"No. Gods no." Solomon's balls were right there in his face and Azil wasted no more time. He licked and sucked them as he began to jerk Solomon off. Solomon kept himself steady with a hand to Azil's head and one to his other shoulder. He made the most enticing sounds as Azil pleasured him.

Azil slid a finger down Solomon's crack to tease at his pucker.

"Yes," Solomon hissed, bucking his hips.

"The lube." Azil had to stop and find it. He did so quickly. "Open it." He held it up to Solomon.

Solomon took the cap off then poured some on Azil's fingers. "Your dick, let me slick it up."

Azil hated having to let go of Solomon. He'd have hated not being able to sink his cock into the silky heat of his ass even more. Azil wiggled until he got the sweats off. His feet were bare. No one wore shoes in the clan so there were none to borrow.

He coated his shaft liberally, using the rest of the little tube of liquid. "Now come back here."

"Gladly." Solomon hitched his leg up again, presenting his genitals to Azil.

Azil rubbed his fingers over Solomon's hole. With just a little pressure, the tip went in easy enough. Then Azil licked up Solomon's balls to his cock. He looked into Solomon's eyes and opened his mouth.

Solomon fed Azil his cock in increments as Azil fingered Solomon's hole. When Solomon's pucker loosened up enough, Azil inserted a second finger, then a third.

"So good, honey. Gods, so good." Solomon pushed into Azil's throat and moaned, a long, low sound that conveyed intense pleasure. Azil swallowed and wiggled his fingers, but the angle was wrong and he couldn't get deep enough to caress Solomon's gland — not that he seemed to mind. Solomon rocked back, riding Azil's digits, then forward again to sink his dick into Azil's mouth.

Azil sucked Solomon's length like it was his only source of oxygen. He let Solomon control the rest, the moving and thrusting, the speed and depth. Azil gave himself to his mate and Solomon didn't abuse him by shoving in carelessly and hurting Azil's throat.

"Now, please, Azil. Let me ride you now," Solomon rasped, pulling out of Azil's mouth. "I want to come on your cock."

That was exactly what Azil wanted, too. "Come here." He scooted back a few feet then sprawled.

Solomon was on him in a hot minute, kneeling over Azil and holding Azil's cock up. "Finally," Solomon said. He began to lower himself onto Azil's shaft. "Gods, gods, honey—" Solomon undulated his hips, then seated himself fully.

"Solomon!" Azil arched, thrusting up instinctively. "Sol!" He couldn't think past the blinding pleasure cause by that sudden, total immersion into Solomon's entrance.

"Yes, yes, yes," Solomon began to rasp as he started moving. He placed his hands on Azil's chest.

"Love this position. Love you." Azil hoped he got the right words out. It was easier to just make sure Solomon could feel him, feel the love and need and ecstasy Azil let flow into their mate link.

Solomon cried out and rose up faster, came down harder.

Azil reached for Solomon's dick, jacking him just as hard, just as fast.

When Solomon came, the relief in his breathless cry was a something Azil would treasure forever. He dropped down and kissed Azil sloppily before sitting up and grinding his butt against Azil's groin.

Azil was lost. His climax hit him and tore through him, spreading bliss and warmth throughout his body.

Solomon eventually bent and gave him another wet kiss. "You do the best things to me."

Azil ran his hands over Solomon's thighs. He realized he'd just spread spunk when he did so. "Sorry. For the cum on you, not for doing the best things to you. I'll never be sorry for that."

"Better not be." Solomon squeezed his buttocks, giving Azil's cock a mind-boggling massage. "Think we can go again? We've got at least a half hour left. You could roll me over and just have your way with me."

Which sounded like the best idea Azil had heard all day, so he did just that.

# Epilogue

They stood looking at the new home. It was three-story, painted a soft yellow with a pale blue door, porch and shutters. The roof was red Saltillo tile. The place was almost twice the size of their old one.

"The stairs will keep us fit." Solomon groped Azil's butt. "Not that I've got any complaints. You've got a perfect bottom."

Azil wiggled it then grabbed a handful of Solomon's. "You too. Shifters stay in good shape anyway. I'm thinking the stairs might be a tool to utilize in wearing kids out for bedtime."

"They'll all be sliding down them in sleeping bags," Solomon said drolly. "You know the kids. Everything's a ride."

"Except for the broom, mop, vacuum, or any other cleaning tool. Those are all anathema. Possibly even toxic, depending on the chore and which kid you ask." Azil held up a finger. "And Dmitri can't clean without breaking something. At least it's usually a glass or dish and not one of his bones. I can't decide if he's doing it on purpose because he thinks we'll quit assigning him chores, or if he's just clumsy."

"I think he's careless. Just doesn't pay attention because he's got other stuff going on in his head. He's always on cloud nine," Solomon explained. Dmitri was creative, and he often was too busy thinking up ideas and drawings and stories instead of paying attention to the here and now.

"He can write plays for Shaun and his acting troupe," Azil offered. "I still can't believe he's really considering doing that."

"It started off as a joke, but Shaun could do it. A few people might even come to see him and whoever else acts with him." Solomon couldn't hold back a snicker. "Hopefully no one will throw tomatoes at him."

Azil frowned. "Why would they throw tomatoes?"

"As a sign that they don't like what they're watching." Solomon shrugged. "I don't even know if that ever really happened. Seems like something people would do. Gods know I want to chunk tomatoes or bricks at the TV sometimes."

"Read books. Most of them are better. I have gotten some with endings that make me angry, but I just read another one and get over it." Azil rubbed his hands together. "I love the eReader you gave me. It's my favorite possession. I'm going to buy so many books I'll need two eReaders." He frowned again. "Right after I figure out how I'm going to earn money. I was thinking about babysitting. Would that be too much? Watch kids so their parents could run for a few hours?"

"Eh." Solomon thought it over. "I don't see what it'd hurt. Just have them bring the kids here. We'll have plenty of room, and we sure have plenty of kids, though, dang. They're growing up so fast."

"I'll think about it before doing it. There has to be more to consider, like feeding them, how much to charge, stuff like that. I'll research it online." Azil leaned against him. "The kids might be growing up fast, but they're also growing up good. You are an amazing man, my mate."

"I had help. Still do." Solomon looked down at his shoes. They were worn leather boots, the toes scuffed to bits, but he loved those boots.

Azil gave his arm a tug. "You didn't at first, and those formative years with kids are very important. You shaped them into being good kids from the start. Look at Rhea now. Once you sat down and worked with her about her fears of being abandoned, she's done so much better."

"I still think we should look for her mom. Rhea says no now, but in another few years, she might change her mind. If I can at least get a name and a clan or lepe, then when that time comes, I'll have answers for her." Solomon had started trying to trace the parentage of each child. The mother's side, anyways. It wasn't easy. He'd had no success so far. That didn't mean he'd give up.

"That's a good idea." Azil looked at the house again. "I just can't get over this. It's so big, so perfect for us."

Solomon had to agree. "I'm glad we have the apartments over the garage, and the cottages out back. Our family's getting bigger with Elena and her mate, and the twins, Erdwin, Kylie—they could all find their mates, too, and stay here if they want. *If* they want." He could let them go. Solomon would do what was best for them, not what he wanted. He wouldn't be a clingy, sobbing mess. He hoped.

Azil hugged him. "You'll do fine. That one room, right by ours. That's going to be a nursery, isn't it?"

They hadn't discussed it specifically, but... "Yes. You and I are just starting out, but someday, if you want to get started on that dozen kids Remus blessed us with, we could use the room for a nursery for sure."

"Why wait?"

Solomon stared at Azil.

Azil frowned. "Seriously, why wait? We've got a houseful of kids now. The age gap between the youngest and a newborn will be large. We could check into that orphanage in Colorado, see if we could bring home some kids that are maybe too old for a nursery, but still needing a family."

"You mean that?" Solomon asked, his stomach quivering, and his heart expanding with love. "You don't care if they're babies or not. Of course you wouldn't. You love all these wild things, and none of them are babies."

"Babies are really small," Azil muttered. "If we're going to have them, we could work our way down to them. I'd be scared to hold a newborn, or even one that couldn't walk yet. Not sure I'd be good with them."

"You'd be fabulous with any age," Solomon said. "You've got a big heart, just like I do. We can love every child we have."

Azil smiled. "We could make it a road trip with Remus and Cliff. You know Cliff wants kids. Rhea has adopted him, but he looks so sad every time she takes her dolls and comes home."

Solomon did know that. "I think it's just that he misses the dolls. I don't know why he threw the one I bought him. At me. Threw it at me. Talk about ungrateful."

"I saw him playing with it yesterday, with Rhea of course. He must have picked it back up."

"I think it's funny he makes such a fuss about it all. I still play dolls with Rhea, and I've played dolls and makeup with the girls." Solomon pushed back a strand of hair from his eyes. At least his hair was growing back quickly. So was Azil's. "Erdwin's taken over makeup duty. Kylie loves the race cars."

"We have a good family." Azil licked his lips. "And right now, they're all busy shopping and playing with their friends. We could break in our new bedroom."

"That sounds like an excellent plan." Solomon took Azil's hand. "One we should act on. Immediately." They laughed and ran to the house. Solomon opened the front door then scooped Azil into his arms. "Wait. This is weird. You want to carry me over the threshold instead?"

"Why are we doing this?" Azil asked, holding onto him.

"It's a thing. Supposed to be romantic. The groom carries the bride over the threshold after they marry and go to their new house." Solomon started to set Azil down. "But we're both guys, grooms, however you want to put it, so... Weird."

"Don't put me down. I think it's romantic. I like romantic stuff." Azil nuzzled his chest. "And I'll carry you over the back door threshold, or the bedroom, somewhere. We'll figure it out later."

"Sounds like a plan to me." Solomon lifted Azil a little higher. "At least our bed is here. Thank goodness." He carried Azil into the bedroom, still on the ground floor. Numerous smoke detectors were in place, something else they'd failed to have at their prior residence. Bobby had made them mandatory in every home. Remus had been irritated with them being installed in his. Bobby had told him to suck it up.

Solomon put Azil on the bed. "Now, you're all mine."

"I am always all yours," Azil retorted.

Solomon nodded. "And I'm yours." He trotted back to lock the bedroom door. "Better safe than interrupted."

"I agree." Azil quickly undressed.

Solomon did the same then he pounced onto the bed. "Gimme." He pulled Azil into his arms. He kissed Azil's cheeks, his jaw, then took a deep, deep taste of his mate, sealing his lips over Azil's. When he'd mapped out every bit of Azil's mouth, Solomon began nibbling his way down.

"Oh, gods," Azil moaned as Solomon licked his neck. Solomon did love the sounds his mate made during pleasure.

"I think I'll mark you right..." He dragged his tongue over down to Azil's bare chest, stopping right above his left nipple. "Here."

"Please," Azil rasped, cupping Solomon's head. "Do it. I want you to mark me now."

That Azil was already pleading for a bite, without Solomon having done more than some kissing and cuddling with his mate, thrilled Solomon. He loved knowing that he turned Azil on so much. Azil certainly affected him the same way.

Solomon took the time to caress every bit of Azil that he was able to reach, because there was no way he couldn't touch Azil's bare skin when he was lying nude and writhing on their bed. "You know how much I love you?" he asked, even though he knew the answer. Azil was giving him everything, so much more than just his physical self. He always did.

"Yes. As much as I love you. Now come here." Azil tugged and Solomon came back up to sip kisses from his lips.

When Azil was squirming and rutting against him, Solomon moved down again. His own dick was hard as steel, but he wasn't going to come yet. He fisted Azil's cock, already wet-tipped. Solomon stroked down, then up, and Azil keened, planting his heels on the bed and thrusting up. Solomon marked him then, striking fast. Azil's flavor was tangy and sweet, the sounds he made musical and broken as he spilled his seed over Solomon's hand.

Solomon sucked the wound until he'd stroked away the last of Azil's climax. He gently disengaged his teeth from Azil's flesh then cleaned the wound with lips and tongue. Azil's cock barely softened beneath him. Solomon could feel the connection thrumming, growing even more as it did every day, passing back and forth between them.

Strengthening with every single beat of their hearts.

"Come here," Azil said again a moment later. Solomon did, coming up to receive more kisses. Azil moaned into his mouth and locked his arms around Solomon's shoulders. "In me, Solomon."

Solomon wasn't a fool, and his heart was full of love for his mate, full of tenderness and desire. "I'm so lucky to have you," Solomon whispered. "I love you. I'll love our family. We're going to be happy for a long time."

*"We will,"* Azil agreed silently. *"I love you, too. I'm glad we can be your family."*

Solomon's eyes burned and he blinked rapidly as he buried his face against Azil's neck. The smell of the man was such an aphrodisiac, Solomon shivered. Then he began making his way down Azil's body again, worshiping every inch of that soft, bare skin he could reach. Both of Azil's nipples were brought to taut peaks, the skin darkened and heated from Solomon's attentions. Solomon ran his hands over Azil's arms, and down his sides. Silky skin, smooth muscles that contracted when he stroked them—the man was sheer perfection.

Azil parted his legs wider, begging with his body, pushing at Solomon's shoulders, but Solomon wouldn't be rushed. He licked every line, every dip and crevice, driving more and more needy sounds from Azil. Solomon dipped his tongue into Azil's belly button and Azil squirmed, laughing sharply. "Stop! No! Don't!"

Solomon knew what his mate meant. He moved down farther, lipping the light trail of hair leading to the thicker patch surrounding Azil's cock. Long and fat, nicely veined, Solomon would never tire of it. He ringed the base with finger and thumb then stopped tormenting them both. He sucked the crown in, licking at the wet slit at the same time.

Azil jolted, and Solomon hefted his sac with his other hand. Silky and smooth, there was no hair on Azil's balls. Solomon liked that, a lot. He took Azil's cock in further, using every technique he knew to drive Azil mad with need. When Azil's cock was in his throat, Solomon thumbed over Azil's hole.

"Yes," Azil hissed, driving his buttocks down.

Solomon had to come back up before he had with more cock than he could handle. He laved Azil's crown for a moment, still teasing that softly wrinkled skin below.

"Please," Azil begged.

Solomon came off his dick with a wet slurp. He couldn't resist tonguing the slit again before meeting Azil's gaze. "Lube."

Azil tossed it at him almost before the word was out. Solomon caught it and chuckled at Azil's eagerness, though he understood it perfectly. He uncapped the lube and coated his fingers and dick. After that, he didn't care where the little container landed when he tossed it aside. Solomon curled Azil's hips up and had his ass in the air, was moving, bending, licking over the furled skin he'd teased with his thumb.

Azil whimpered and reached for his cock. He gripped it tight, as if holding back his second release. Solomon closed his eyes as he rimmed Azil, losing himself in pure enjoyment of pleasing his mate. When he had Azil's hole soaked and open enough for his tongue to easily slip in and out, Solomon came up and slid two fingers into the tight channel.

"So hot," Solomon gritted out, feeling that vise-like grip around his digits. "Soft and..." Oh gods, he probably wasn't going to last long enough to make a good impression.

"You will," Azil said. "Now. Now, Solomon."

Solomon lowered Azil's butt down and moved into position between his legs. He lined his cock up and began to push in, his gaze shooting up to Azil's.

There was so much that he felt just then, and none of it describable with any words he knew. Everything of Solomon's was about Azil, his heart, his mind, his soul. Solomon was enveloped in his mate's body and spirit. Slowly, he sank deeper, Azil's body drawing him in.

Azil's lashes fluttered, his lips parted. "Solomon," he whispered.

Instead of the rushed coupling he'd feared giving in to, Solomon made love to his mate with tender strokes, memorizing every sound, every flicker of Azil's eyes, his mouth, his expression. Over and over, he withdrew, only to be welcomed back into Azil's warm embrace.

When he came, his climax tangled with Azil's, both of them gasping, eyes locked on the other, perfect synchronicity between them. Solomon's cock pulsed, emptying into Azil.

There was no need for words. They were bound as one, the Fates having brought them together, knowing the needs of the one for the other, the perfect matches they had designed in Solomon and Azil.

# About the Author

A native Texan, Bailey spends her days spinning stories around in her head, which has contributed to more than one incident of tripping over her own feet. Evenings are reserved for pounding away at the keyboard, as are early morning hours. Sleep? Doesn't happen much. Writing is too much fun, and there are too many characters bouncing about, tapping on Bailey's brain demanding to be let out.

Caffeine and chocolate are permanent fixtures in Bailey's office and are never far from hand at any given time. Removing either of those necessities from Bailey's presence can result in what is know as A Very, Very Scary Bailey and is not advised under any circumstances.

Bailey Bradford loves to hear from readers. You can find her contact information, website details and author profile page at http://www.totallybound.com.

Totally Bound Publishing